P9-EEI-726
3 1833 04692 7635

Slade Stanfield

"I was reckless, and now Susannah can't walk, let alone climb hills." He looked around at all the hills they'd once climbed together as children. His heart clenched at the reality. "How does someone forgive himself for such an atrocity?"

Isabel stopped, and he followed suit, though he didn't turn and face her. He kept his eyes on the brown and yellow earth beneath his feet.

"I don't know, Slade. I don't know." She laid a hand on his arm. "I only know locking her away isn't the answer." Her hushed tone carried compassion and tenderness.

"I don't want anything to hurt her, not ever again."

"Neither do I. Neither does your mother." Isabel moved around in front of him and took hold of his hands. "But none of us has that sort of control over another's life. People we love get hurt. I don't know why, but I've lived long enough to know it is so."

All his anger had faded, and what Isabel said almost made sense. His well-meaning plan to keep Susannah safe and to control her environment was being blown to bits by one determined, fiery-haired woman. He made the mistake of looking up into those green eyes, and he forgot how much he disliked her, forgot how headstrong she was, and forgot everything except her lips. Those he couldn't forget, and he inched his way toward them.

SEP 01 2004

JERI ODELL is a native of Tucson, Arizona. She and husband Dean celebrated thirty years of marriage last summer. They are the parents of three wonderful adult children. Jeri holds family dear to her heart, second only to God. This is Jeri's fourth novel for **Heartsong Presents**. She's also written four novellas and articles on family issues for several Christian publications and a nonfiction book. She thanks God for the privilege of writing for Him. For more information on her or her books go to www.jeriodell.com. You may email her at jeri@jeriodell.com.

Books by Jeri Odell

HEARTSONG PRESENTS

HP413—Remnant of Victory
HP467—Hidden Treasures
HP525—Game of Pretend

Don't miss out on any of our super romances. Write to us at the following address for information on our newest releases and club information.

Heartsong Presents Readers' Service
PO Box 719
Uhrichsville, OH 44683

Or check out our Web site at www.heartsongpresents.com

Surrendered Heart

Jeri Odell

Heartsong Presents

For Adam & Melissa:
May God always find your hearts surrendered to Him, and may He bless your May 28 wedding day with His presence and His love.

And for Anna W. & Elise Y.—thanks for being two special teenagers and encouraging me to tell Isabel's story. I hope you enjoy her tale.

A note from the Author:
I love to hear from my readers! You may correspond with me by writing:

Jeri Odell
Author Relations
PO Box 719
Uhrichsville, OH 44683

ISBN 1-59310-118-X

SURRENDERED HEART

Copyright © 2004 by Jeri Odell. All rights reserved. Except for use in any review, the reproduction or utilization of this work in whole or in part in any form by any electronic, mechanical, or other means, now known or hereafter invented, is forbidden without the permission of Heartsong Presents, an imprint of Barbour Publishing, Inc., PO Box 719, Uhrichsville, Ohio 44683.

Our mission is to publish and distribute inspirational products offering exceptional value and biblical encouragement to the masses.

All Scripture quotations are taken from the King James Version of the Bible.

All of the characters and events in this book are fictitious. Any resemblance to actual persons, living or dead, or to actual events is purely coincidental.

PRINTED IN THE U.S.A.

one

September 1883

Standing in line before boarding the train, Isabel Fairchild raised her gaze, taking in the foggy San Francisco sky. Her pulse raced. *I'm leaving! I'm actually leaving!* At last, she was free. Free to find her way in the world. Free to find independence and adventure. Free from marrying a man her father deemed good for her. A man less exciting than milk toast. No, she would never be Mrs. Horace A. Peabody, no matter how much her father desired the match.

She couldn't help smiling. At the top of the steps, she paused and turned, taking one last gander at the city of her birth. Isabel sucked in a deep breath, savoring the moist sea air. "I will not miss this place," she whispered. "I will not miss a family who cannot accept me for who I am." *Well, perhaps I shall miss them a little.*

"Miss, I need your ticket." The conductor held out his hand. "You're holding up the procession."

"Yes, please." Several people behind her, also waiting, agreed.

Isabel flashed her most charming smile at the crowd following her and at the railroad employee—the smile that worked on all men. "I'm so sorry, sir." She riffled through her satchel and handed him her ticket. "I longed for one last peek because I'll never be back. I didn't mean you any trouble." She tilted her head toward the right, just so.

The conductor's annoyed expression melted away. "Why, you're no trouble at all, miss." He tipped his hat, and she moved forward into the train car. Securing a window seat, Isabel shoved her satchel underneath. She brought very little with her, since she'd sneaked out of the house. After all, this was the beginning of a new life, and she wanted all things new, including her clothes.

"Excuse me, ma'am, is this seat taken?"

"Why, no, and I'd be honored if you used it." Isabel held the full skirt of her dress close so the older gentleman could settle in beside her.

"Name's Ronald Tripp, ma'am." He removed his hat and nodded his head.

"Nice meeting you, Mr. Tripp. I'm Miss Isabel Fairchild."

"Where are you headed, Miss Fairchild?"

Something about his keen eyes made Isabel uncomfortable, so she kept her answer short. "Arizona."

"Me, too." He nodded his silver head. "Going to Phoenix, myself. How about you?"

"No, not Phoenix." Isabel pulled her bag out and dug through for the letter she'd written her family. Perhaps if she were reading, this man would let her alone. She unfolded the letter and reread her words for about the tenth time.

Dearest Mother and Father,

I'm writing so you will know I am safe and en route to Tombstone, Arizona. I've accepted a respectable job there.

She doubted her family would consider a dancer in a saloon respectable, so she didn't mention what she'd be doing. Her parents didn't understand her sense of adventure. Didn't understand her at all. Only knew they wanted her to be more like her sister Magdalene. The harder they tried to push, the more she rebelled and chose to be different.

I do love you both and hope you realize I can't possibly marry Mr. Peabody. Nor can I be Magdalene or Gabrielle. There must be more of life than what they've settled for.

Isabel breathed out a wistful sigh. "Although for the chance of becoming Mrs. Chandler Alexandre, I'd have settled for the same."

"I beg your pardon, miss?" Mr. Tripp appeared confused, and his question brought Isabel out of her reminiscing.

"Sorry. I'm thinking aloud." Isabel refolded the letter and tucked it back into the envelope.

"Running from a love gone wrong?"

"Something like that." Isabel stuck the envelope into the pocket of her suit coat.

"Did he marry someone else?"

"None other than my sister."

"Oh, dear girl, what a painful loss."

Isabel nodded. "No man had ever even been interested in Magdalene. I never thought of her as competition."

"Poor lass." Mr. Tripp patted Isabel's hand in a grandfather-like gesture. "Hearts do heal. Time, you need time. You'll meet another."

"There is only one Chandler."

"Ah, too true, but somewhere out there is a lad even better than him. More suited for you. I'm sure 'tis true."

Isabel gazed into his kind gray eyes and smiled. She lifted her chin. "I've given up on love. Life is too short not to live every day. I shall sing and dance and find a wonderful adventure."

"How is your family feelin' about this adventure of yours?"

"They don't know yet. Won't until they get this letter." She patted her pocket. "Why, do you know my father wished I'd marry some man twice my age? But I'll have none of his silliness! This is my life, and I'll not accept Horace A. Peabody as my betrothed!"

"I see your quandary, but fathers, more often than not, fancy the best for their young lassies."

A tiny stab of guilt pricked Isabel's conscience. She'd gotten pretty wild. Her father hoped marrying a respectable man would rein her in. "True enough. He does desire the best for me. We can't agree on what that is, so I took control of my life and am doing this my way."

"I hope things work out and you find the life you're searching for." He set his hat back on his head and rose. "I'm in need of a little rest. The seat behind us is now empty, so I'll be laying myself down."

Isabel smiled. "Good day, Mr. Tripp."

"And good day to you, Miss Fairchild."

Isabel focused her gaze out the window. Her family did want the best for her. She'd embarrassed them with her flirtatious ways, but it was all so harmless. She loved a good party, loved dancing and singing, but so what? And yes, she'd kissed more men than any young woman should have, but again, so what? A little innocent kissing never hurt anyone. She enjoyed men's attention, but what woman didn't?

Isabel glanced back over her seat at Mr. Tripp, wondering if he'd fallen asleep, but the seat sat empty. She considered asking his opinion about kissing without commitment. She shrugged. At his age, he'd side with her father.

❧

Slade Stanfield first noticed the girl with the fiery curls when he waited in line for the train. Something about her tall, slender frame caught a man's eye; something about the graceful, confident way she carried herself held a man's attention; and something about those large, emerald eyes as they gazed over the city sparked a man's interest. Therefore, he planned on avoiding her like a moldy batch of hay, but alas, he boarded last and one seat had remained—the one across the aisle from her.

Certain she wore the latest style, Slade wondered why any sane person would have such an outlandish hat. What woman in her right mind wanted a bird's nest perched on her head? Some old codger had settled in alongside her. The aged fellow got her talking, and Slade learned a lot. Not that he condoned eavesdropping. He couldn't help it; they were an arm's length away. He didn't care to know a thing about her or the details of her life. He shouldn't think about her anyway. No matter how appealing or interesting Miss Isabel Fairchild might be, he'd committed himself to Susannah; he had no room in his life for another woman.

Thoughts of Susannah brought a pang of regret. Would he ever find a suitable companion for her? He'd hoped this trip up the coast to San Francisco would have been fruitful, but the only women interested in being a lame woman's companion were elderly types. He searched for a young woman who'd share a friendship with Susannah. Two years and still no one. He shook his head in frustration and returned to eavesdropping on Miss Fairchild and her problems—then he didn't think about his own.

When the old guy decided on a nap, so did Slade. This went on for hours—talking, napping, eating, listening. When he awoke this time, the conductor announced they were pulling into Los Angeles.

Miss Fairchild stretched and yawned across the aisle. Their

gazes met. She smiled, and he knew any man was clay in her hands. Earlier he'd shaken his head at the way she'd used her beauty for manipulating the conductor. Now he realized how effortlessly he could fall under her spell. She knew how to look at a man.

As the train slowed, Miss Fairchild reached under the seat for her bag. "My satchel is gone!" Panic laced each word. Next thing he knew, she was crawling on her hands and knees, frantically searching. She checked under the seat in front of her. "Have you seen my bag?" She glanced in Slade's direction. "Perhaps it slid to your side of the train."

Slade doubted the plausibility of such an event transpiring, but he checked under his own seat, the one in front of him, and the one behind him. He found no bag.

The confident, controlled Miss Fairchild seemed terrified. "What will I do? My money, my ticket for Tombstone, everything I own is gone." She sank onto the cushioned seat. "I have nothing except the clothes on my back."

Her fearful expression left Slade feeling concerned; after all, an honorable man didn't abandon a lady in distress. "Let's search the whole car." It had almost emptied out by now. "We'll start at the front. You take your side, and I'll take mine." He offered his hand and helped her up, surprised by the jolt of electricity shooting through him at her touch.

He wished he could assure her they'd find the missing luggage, but in all honesty, he doubted they would. That Mr. Tripp fellow probably absconded with Miss Fairchild's belongings. Maybe this was some kind of scam, and they were in it together. He glanced at her pale, worried face as she checked yet another row. *Why is trust so difficult for me? Maybe she's telling the truth. Or maybe she'll be asking for a loan,* his cynical side argued.

3 1833 04692 7635

Miss Fairchild's face grew more anxious as they searched under seat after seat with no luck. At the back of the car, she appeared near tears but raised her chin, drawing in a determined breath. She was a fighter—that he knew for certain.

"Let me help you find the conductor. We'll see what he advises." Slade took her arm, leading her down the steps. *Don't think about how she smells like the lilac growing down by the barn. Don't think about how fragile and forlorn she all of a sudden seems. Most of all, don't think about those moist green eyes, harboring unshed tears. . . .* Once on the ground, he quickly released her and took a step back. Glancing down the track and then up, he spotted the conductor near the front of the train, speaking with the engineer.

"There he is." Miss Fairchild hiked up her skirts and ran in the opposite direction. "Mr. Tripp, stop! You've got my bag."

Slade spotted the older man, and, sure enough, he carried the satchel Miss Fairchild had boarded with. Slade caught up with her. "Go tell the conductor what has transpired here today." Before she'd had time to respond, he sprinted after the old codger.

Mr. Tripp ducked around another train. Slade cut between cars. He stopped, his breathing ragged. Slade searched in every direction, but the man had vanished. Slade jogged up and down, hunting between the various trains. *How can a man evaporate?* Then he searched the depot, but the man had disappeared into thin air. Discouraged, Slade sought out Miss Fairchild, dreading giving her the bad news.

He found her standing near the depot entrance, looking regal and every bit a lady. "Did you catch him?" she asked in a desperate tone.

"No, I'm sorry. I didn't." Slade took another glimpse in each direction.

The conductor approached. "I'm sorry, miss. We searched every train. He isn't to be found."

She swallowed hard. "Can the railroad replace my ticket?"

The conductor shook his head. "Only if you pay for another one."

Isabel took a deep breath. She placed her hand on the conductor's arm. "Surely an important man such as yourself could do something." She licked her lips and tilted her head to the right. "I'm just asking one tiny little favor." Holding her thumb and forefinger about an inch apart, she illustrated what a tiny bit of help she requested.

She had the poor man right where she wanted him. He patted the hand perched on his arm. "I'll go check and see what I can do."

Isabel batted her eyes, long lashes making the action all the more appealing. "Thank you so much. I'm certain a man in your position can take care of this for me."

With his chest puffed out so that he resembled a strutting rooster, he tipped his hat and walked toward the station.

Miss Fairchild turned toward Slade, her green eyes assessing him—eyes a man could drown in. Laying her hand on his arm, she said, "We've not been properly introduced."

Her touch sped up the beat of his heart. "Name's Stanfield. Slade Stanfield." Pulling away from her, he removed his hat and ducked his head.

"It's a pleasure to meet you, Mr. Stanfield. I'm Isabel Fairchild." She stretched out her arm, expecting him to kiss her hand. Well, he had news for her; he'd not be clay in her hands like that foolish conductor. Besides, he needed his wits about him, and being near her shattered them, so he ignored her outstretched arm and searched the area one last time, still not seeing any sign of Mr. Tripp.

"Anyway," Miss Fairchild recovered quickly from his rejection, "I cannot thank you enough for all your kindness toward me."

The conductor reappeared, making a response to Miss Fairchild avoidable. Slade knew by his sheepish look, he'd failed to fulfill Miss Fairchild's request.

"Miss, I'm so sorry, but nothing can be done by the railroad. According to the station agent, you were responsible to see to your own belongings." He kept his eyes focused on the hat in his hands rather than look at her when he delivered the news.

Miss Fairchild stomped her slender foot. "If you did not allow thieves and scoundrels to ride your railroad, this never would have happened! I am now penniless, and you have not heard the last of me!"

The poor man backed a step away with each word she spat at him. "I must get to my train. It's due to leave soon." He turned and bolted.

"Can you believe that man had the audacity to imply this is somehow my fault? How could I have known that Mr. Tripp was a less than honorable man?" Isabel shone her brightest smile on him. "Mr. Stanfield, you seem like a kind and reasonable man. A gentleman who wouldn't possibly leave a lady stranded in Los Angeles with no money and no belongings."

She wasn't about to play him for a fool. "Miss Fairchild—"

"Please, you must call me Isabel."

Her hand was back on his arm, wreaking havoc with his senses. *Don't think about how soft her skin is. Don't think about the fear in her eyes. Don't think about her at all.*

"Slade—may I call you Slade?"

"You don't need to call me anything. In five minutes, I'll be on the train to San Diego, and we will never lay eyes on one another again." The words came out sounding as harsh as he'd intended, and they affected Miss Fairchild. Her confidence eroded some, and she removed her hand from his arm. He was thankful for that. Now maybe he could think clearly.

"I'm sorry to have offended you." Her chin quivered, and tears pooled in her eyes. "I only hoped you'd loan me the money to get to Arizona. I would have repaid you in full, plus interest. Forgive my intrusion on your time."

With those words, Isabel Fairchild walked away. Only Slade couldn't help but notice the slump of her shoulders and the defeat in her step.

Maybe I should loan her the money, but then again, maybe it's all a scam. Maybe I could offer her a job. After all, I need a companion for Susannah. But with this intense attraction to her, that might not be such a good idea, and what if she really is a crook? If she's a crook, she won't take the job. She'll find someone to give her cash.

All the good sense he'd ever possessed melted away when he thought of what might happen to her if he left her there—what she might be forced to do to earn her passage. But having Isabel Fairchild underfoot day in and day out could wear a man down. With either decision, he wasn't sure he could live with himself.

❧

"I will not cry. I will not cry. I will not cry." Isabel sauntered toward the train station like a woman without a care in the world, whispering the reminder with each step. Taking deep breaths, she attempted to squelch the fear that rose inside. What if no one would help her? Had she lost her ability to get a man to do her bidding?

I'll sit down and compose myself. I'll find someone to loan me the money. I will not let my plans go by the wayside because of one man. Oh, that Slade Stanfield. She'd never met a man immune to her charms until this year. Now, she'd met two. First Chandler and now Slade. Well, she'd not give him another thought. She reached for the depot door handle.

"Miss Fairchild! Isabel."

Well, well, well, he wasn't immune to her after all! She fought a smug smile. It wouldn't do at all for him to see her gloat. Instead, she adopted a sad and forlorn expression before turning to face him.

He hustled toward her. "Miss Fairchild, I cannot offer you money, but I can, however, offer you a job."

"A job? A respectable job?" What might he be suggesting?

"Much more respectable than a dance-hall girl."

"How dare you condemn me?" He sounded just like her father. "I may want to dance and sing, but it's not as though I'd work in a brothel. I have my standards."

"I'm sorry. I didn't mean to insult you. Come sit with me inside, and we'll discuss my proposition."

Proposition? She didn't like the sound of that at all. After she settled her skirts, her bustle, and herself onto the bench, Slade joined her.

"Miss Fairchild, I have a lame sister who is begging me to hire a companion about her age. I've searched the whole state of California but have yet to find someone suitable."

"And you find me suitable?" Isabel doubted that.

"Let's just say I find you in need of a job, so I'm offering you one, if you are willing to accept to my terms."

"What terms?" Would he expect her to be his mistress? She fidgeted with one of the large buttons on her suit coat.

"You come with me to my ranch in San Diego and live there for six months—"

Isabel shot up off the train station bench. She spun to face him, arms crossed in vexation. "Mr. Stanfield, I will not live on your ranch and be your mistress for six months." Her voice was louder than she'd intended, and several people turned to stare.

two

Slade jumped up off the bench. "Miss Fairchild, I assure you I have no interest in you except as a companion for my younger sister."

His rejection stung. Isabel was used to having men respond to her in a more positive light.

"And even in that capacity, you are probably a bad choice." His words poured out in a clipped, exasperated tone. "Now will you please sit down and refrain from further outbursts?"

Both returned to their previous spots on the seat. How could he say she'd be a bad choice as a companion? And how did he find her so unappealing? Looking at his grim expression, she refrained from asking.

"Miss Fairchild, I am offering you a six-month stint at my ranch as my lame sister's companion. She's very lonely. At the end of that time, I will pay your passage to Tombstone and give you a small stipend to boot."

Isabel chewed her bottom lip and weighed her options. This was only a minor setback. Maybe even an unplanned adventure. Yes, in six months she'd be back on course, boarding a train for Tombstone, *or maybe I should find someone else to loan me the money.* She glanced around the station. Every man was with a lady or a family. She didn't see anyone traveling alone with whom she could flirt, charm, and borrow money from. Her gaze returned to Slade. His slate gray eyes stared into her soul, and she squirmed under his scrutiny.

"You think you can find a better offer?" He, too, glanced

around the room and rose. "Your decision." He shrugged one shoulder as if he couldn't care less which one she made.

The panic and fear returned. "Wait. I'll go with you for six months." She held out her hand to seal the deal, just the way she'd seen her father do. Her father. She reached in her pocket and pulled out the letter to her parents. "Will you loan me the postage for this? You can deduct it from my pay at the end of the six months."

Slade reached for the envelope and nodded. "Wait here." He made his way to the station agent behind the counter. He exchanged cash for her ticket and left the envelope with the man as well, then returned to Isabel. "Our train leaves soon." Slade offered her his arm; Isabel accepted it, and he led her to the correct line. "I paid the man extra for mailing your letter."

"Thank you."

"Isabel, I want you to understand a few things." His bleak expression tied her stomach in knots. "You must abide by my rules since you'll be living under my roof for the next six months."

Her father had said those same words to her. She was running from rules to freedom, and now she was right back where she started. "What are your rules?"

He placed his hand on the small of her back, propelling her forward with the rest of the line and sending goose bumps up her spine at the same time. "Neither you nor my sister may leave the house at any time unless accompanied."

"Why?"

"Isabel, I don't owe you an explanation. You work for me—therefore, you abide by my rules." The pulse in his jaw throbbed, and Isabel knew this must be a heated subject.

They'd reached the front of the line and climbed the steps into the train car. Slade handed the conductor their tickets and led Isabel to the nearest empty bench. He waited for her to situate herself next to the window before he settled beside her.

"My sister will most likely adore you. She's a sweet girl who's wishing for a friend. I expect you to show the utmost integrity when dealing with her. She doesn't need to know your sole ambition is to dance for men in some outlaw-infested town."

Isabel bristled at his description. "If your opinion of me is so low, why would you offer me the job of your sister's caretaker? And for your information, I happen to come from a well-known and upstanding Christian family."

"Isabel, coming from a Christian family doesn't make you a Christian. It doesn't even mean you live by your family's moral code. It only means you grew up going to church and have probably had some exposure to the Bible."

Now she was incensed. "I will have you know my father read us the Bible every night before we knelt for prayer." *But he pressed too hard for me to believe the words. Made me that much more resistant.* The train jerked forward and Isabel's heart sank. *What have I done? I'm committed to this man for six months.*

"Mr. Stanfield, I have no choice but to honor your wishes for the next six months as long as they are not illegal or immoral. After that time, I assure you I will be gone as fast as possible. Until then, we must tolerate each other, but you have no right making assumptions about me or my family."

"I agree, Miss Fairchild. I'd prefer that my sister not know there is tension between us. As for assumptions, time will tell—time will tell." The sure line of his mouth made Isabel desire to wipe the smug expression off his chiseled face.

"Then perhaps you must treat me with kindness instead of disdain."

"And perhaps you will learn respect for authority and submission to rules."

They sat together in silence, watching the miles roll by, and Isabel wondered if she'd just made a deal she'd live to regret. Well, even so, she'd not let him ruin six good months of her life. She'd just make the best of this, she would.

❧

Neither spoke again until the train stopped. Isabel spent the ride looking out the window, and Slade was sure she wished she'd been more careful with her things. Then she wouldn't be in this grand mess and neither would he. If Slade could stay angry with her for the duration, he might be able to avoid dealing with his attraction to her, and staying angry seemed plausible since she constantly irritated him.

Somehow, someway he must keep his distance. Being near her made him ache, ache with wanting things he could never have. Things like a wife, children, even just a life. . .

"My buckboard is at the livery stable. We'll have to walk over there." He took her arm and guided her off the train. He wasn't about to let her out of his sight.

"Surely, you don't expect me to walk. Wouldn't a gentleman allow me to wait here? That is, if you are a gentleman." She raised her brow in a silent challenge, and he knew she hoped to goad him into giving in.

He grasped her elbow in determination. "I think I'd like you by my side, if you don't mind." He led her out of the stuffy station into a sunny San Diego day.

Isabel stopped. "And if I do mind?"

His anger flared. "Isabel, you were bought and paid for, and for the next six months, I hope you'll remember that."

She raised her chin. "A bond servant?"

"If you must view it that way, then yes. You are mine until you work off your debt." He cringed inwardly at his cold, heartless words. "You have no rights except any I choose to give you. Now come on. Time's wasting." He tugged on her arm, but she remained firmly planted.

"You don't trust me."

"No, I don't." *Why should I?*

Isabel stomped her foot. "I am an honest and honorable person. I may be wilder than my family approves of, wilder than you think is proper, but I do have integrity. You paid my passage, and I gave you my word. That should be enough."

He knew he'd offended her—again. "It's not, Isabel. I don't even know you. How can I trust your word?" *And trust is always an issue for me. Trusting people, trusting God. . .*

"So for the next six months, are you going to handcuff me to yourself so I don't escape?" She folded her arms across her midsection.

He sighed, bent his head back, and stared into the sky. *Lord, I realize You continually try to show me, reminding me I have no control. I simply never learn the lesson, do I?*

"Okay, Isabel. I'm about to find out if you are a woman of your word." He walked away, leaving her standing in the middle of the road, a determined angle to her chin. Would she still be there when he returned with the buckboard? He wasn't sure, but something about her passionate declaration convinced him she would, and even if she weren't, maybe her leaving would be best. She was on his mind too often, even though he'd only known her a short while.

Upon his return, Slade spotted Isabel on the bench in front of the train station. A part of him felt relieved. At least she was a woman of her word. Maybe he could trust her with Susannah, after all. Just maybe. . .

Isabel smiled when he stopped the buckboard in front of the depot. Oh, that smile. "Surprised?" she asked, tilting her head in that coy way of hers.

"A little." His heart softened toward her as the tiniest seed of trust planted itself there. He climbed down and lifted her up by her tiny waist. Her mouth, mere inches from his, beckoned for his attention. He swallowed hard the urge to kiss her and instead walked around the horses to the other side and climbed up next to her on the hard wooden seat, putting as much distance between them as he could.

"This is my first ride on a buckboard."

"They aren't known for comfort. You may be disappointed."

"Doubtful. It's a new adventure."

"Ah, Miss Fairchild, the girl that is always in search of an adventure."

She smiled up at him, and her green eyes danced with mischief and excitement. At that moment, he realized Isabel Fairchild didn't just live life—she embraced it. Maybe he could learn a thing or two from her. His life had become pretty mundane and ordinary. He'd lost his zest.

"I've decided to make this whole six months an adventure. After all, I've never lived on a ranch or helped a lame girl. So this will all be new and exciting for me."

Slade bridled at her declaration. He wanted to lecture her that being lame wasn't any sort of adventure and ranch life was more hard work than anything, but he figured he'd been hard enough on her this trip. She'd figure out soon enough how wrong she was. "I need to stop at a couple of places and load up on supplies. First, we'll stop at the hardware store and then the grocers."

A couple of hours later, the buckboard was loaded to overflowing, and they were on their way. Isabel noticed every detail of her surroundings, often asking questions or making observations.

"Where is your ranch located?"

"North of San Diego. It's set in the most beautiful valley this side of heaven." His voice echoed his love for the place.

"What's it like living on a ranch?"

"You, Miss Fairchild, will have to wait and live the adventure for yourself."

She nodded her agreement. "Where is all the green? Why is the whole world yellow and brown?"

"It's the color of September, and September is a time for waiting. Waiting for the rains to bring new grass, waiting between harvesting the corn and planting the oats, waiting for spring to bring a new batch of wildflowers. Even the livestock are waiting for their young to be born."

"In September I start waiting for Thanksgiving and Christmas, for parties and dances."

He grinned and shook his head. "There are no parties and dances out here, Isabel," he warned. "Just a lot of hard work."

"Then we'll make our own party, Mr. Stanfield." She seemed determined not to let him discourage her. "How about you, Mr. Stanfield? What are you waiting for?"

For you, Isabel. I've waited my whole life for you or someone like you, but it's no longer meant to be. How could he go on with his life when he'd robbed Susannah of the chance to go on with hers? "I'm not waiting for anything, Miss Fairchild. I have all I need, all I want."

"Then I'd say you're a lucky man. Few can make those claims."

Few indeed. The horses plodded up the narrow, winding road, working hard pulling the weighty wagon behind them. "If you look back over your shoulder, you get a clear view of the ocean." He took his own advice and glanced back at the panoramic scene. The ocean and sky blended together into a horizon of blue.

"It's beautiful. Makes me feel all wistful inside." She had a faraway, dreamy appearance on her beguiling face. They passed a herdsman. "Why does that man have his cattle grazing along the road outside the fence?"

"Saving hay is money in the bank to a rancher. By utilizing the food nature provides along the roadway, he can save his hay for another day. Out here, a man counts on the seasons and cycles of life. He knows them well." *Those are the only things a man can count on, not people—sometimes not even God.* Slade hated himself for doubting God's goodness, but where had He been when Susannah lost her leg? Where was God when Slade begged Him to heal his sister just hours before the doctor amputated her leg? Where was He today when Slade was being tortured by old dreams he'd long ago buried?

Just before they crested the hill, Slade asked, "Are you ready for your first glimpse of my home—Rancho San Miguel?" He reined the horses to a stop and pointed. "There is the roof of the house down between the sycamore trees and the live oaks. Do you see it over near the river?"

Isabel nodded, not sure what she expected, but certainly nothing so grand. Something about this valley Slade called home tugged her heartstrings. The serene and peaceful place invited her to come, come find what she'd spent her whole life searching for.

No, I won't find it here. I can't find it here. This isn't at all what I want or need. Isabel closed her mind to the possibility. Instead, she focused on her surroundings, drinking in every detail. Wild tobacco and goldenrod grew along the fence. Ground squirrels scampered about, ducking in and out of their burrows.

As the buckboard creaked its way down the path, Isabel squirmed. The jolting and hard seat had grown tiresome. She focused on the house, coming into clear sight now as they descended into the valley.

Slade must have sensed her studying his home. "Looks nothing like San Francisco's three-story, fancy wooden homes, does it?"

"No." The single story had a low, wide veranda. It was made of adobe, which complemented the red tile roof. Ten arches opened the wide porch to the outside world. "But I like it. It's quite charming. It reminds me of the Spanish haciendas I've seen in books."

Slade smiled, and her stomach reacted with a tingling sensation. His gray eyes warmed her. Sometimes his gaze held anger, but sometimes, like this moment, he seemed to admire her. This was the Slade she preferred, not the cool, distant one.

"We'll stop at the house first, and I'll introduce you to Susannah."

Isabel nodded, attempting to swallow her apprehension. She'd never been around lame people before. She wasn't sure how to act. Not always known for her decorum, what if she blurted out something insensitive?

three

"Slade, you're home!" A petite brunette hobbled toward them from one of the archways off the front porch. Slade ran to her, forgetting about Isabel or helping her down from the wagon. He hugged his sister tight, and her carved staff fell forgotten to the ground.

"Susannah, I finally found a companion. Come, I want you to meet Miss Isabel Fairchild." For the first time since Isabel had met him, Slade's smile lit his eyes, and the genuine pleasure he experienced was for his sister.

Slade swung Susannah into his arms and carried her to the buckboard, depositing her next to it so she could hold the wooden side for support. She grinned up at Isabel, still sitting on the inflexible wooden seat. "Isabel, how kind of you to come."

Isabel immediately liked the black-haired beauty with her striking violet eyes and dimples so like her brother's. The old wood of the buckboard creaked beneath her feet when Isabel stood. Slade lifted her down, his strong hands cradling her waist. He was quite handsome now that his sister's presence had erased his brooding expression. His nearness caused Isabel's heart to trip over itself. Must be the excitement of her new adventure, for surely it wasn't his touch; she didn't even like the man, nor he her.

As soon as Slade released her, Isabel turned to his sister. "So good to meet you, Susannah."

"Thank you. I feel exactly the same, and I love your outfit.

Is it the very latest style?" Susannah glanced down at her plain cotton skirt and smiled. "We're not much for fashion out this way." She held her skirt out on one side and laughed.

"I saved all my money to buy this. I wanted to travel in style."

Susannah's brows drew together. "To come to our ranch?"

Great. How do I respond to that? Isabel glanced at Slade, not sure how much to reveal.

"Isabel was actually headed to Arizona when we met. She decided to take a detour and visit the ranch for a few months."

"Only a few months?" Susannah's disappointment was evident.

"Yes. I have a job to get to—"

"Let's not worry about when she'll leave, but enjoy her while she's here." Slade interrupted Isabel—probably afraid she'd say too much. "Why don't you show Isabel the house? She can stay in the room next to yours and will need to borrow some of your things for the duration. Her satchel was stolen."

"Oh, how terrible. You have nothing?" Susannah's forehead crinkled in concern.

"Nothing but this dress, and it seems quite useless on a ranch."

Susannah giggled. "Oh, Isabel, it will be wonderful to have someone to share with. My closet is filled, but I have nothing as grand as your one dress. Now, if you'll stand on my left side and allow me to cling to your arm, I will hobble alongside you. My left leg was amputated just below the knee, and I have a wooden one to replace it, but I still need to lean heavily on someone or something in order to walk."

Susannah's acceptance of her injury made Isabel feel at ease, too. She squeezed between Susannah and the wagon, and Susannah grasped Isabel's upper arm in a tight hold.

Slade tipped his hat. "I'll see you ladies at dinner. Behave, and stay out of trouble." Isabel knew the warning was for her benefit. He climbed back up onto the wagon and tapped the reins against the horses' haunches. The wagon lurched forward toward the barn.

Slowly, Isabel and Susannah tottered toward the house. Isabel stooped to pick up the staff and carried it in her free hand.

"I can't wait for you to meet Mama. You'll take such a load off of her. She's worn out, trying to take care of everything a ranch wife takes care of and care for me as well. Oh, Isabel, I prayed so hard for you." Susannah stopped at the arched opening and hugged her. "You have no idea how grateful I am you came." She loosened her hold, and they continued their slow pace across the long, wide porch.

No one had ever expressed gratitude for Isabel before, and Susannah's attitude brought a lump to her throat. She'd always been the youngest sister everyone shooed away, the younger daughter underfoot and in the way, but here she mattered. Here she could make a difference.

Isabel opened a massive, carved wooden door, and they entered the foyer of the house. The outside walls were almost a foot thick. "This place is a fortress," she commented as they moved across the tile floor.

"Adobe keeps the house cooler in the summer, warmer in the winter," Susannah informed her. They passed through a sitting room and out onto another porch. "As you can see, the house is a U-shape, and every room has a door leading out onto this inner court." Susannah pointed to the wing on the left. "Those are all the bedrooms, and over here. . . ," she said, looking to the right, "is the kitchen, dining hall, parlor, smoking room, and game room."

Isabel took in the grandeur of the place. The portico ran

along all three sides of the house and rested on huge pillars covered by various types of vines. Huge bowls swung by rope from the roof, holding other varieties of flora.

"My mother loves plants and flowers."

Isabel nodded. "I've never seen such large pots." Red clay vessels lined the walls.

"They are actually watering jars made by the Indians, but Mother fills them with her favorite things. These porches are where we live life. Nobody chooses indoors unless the weather forces us to. Mother does all her kitchen work except the actual cooking over there at those tables. Often we sleep on the porches, especially in the hottest days of summer." The love and pride Susannah had for her home shone through her words and expressions.

A small woman came through one of the doors to the right. Her brown skin revealed her Spanish ancestry. "Mama, look who Slade has brought for me! This is Isabel Fairchild, and she'll be visiting with us a few months."

Mrs. Stanfield nodded her gray head and laid her armful of vegetables on a nearby worktable and approached them. "Only a few months?" With eyes black as night, she eyeballed Isabel up and down. "Surely not! My son needs a wife, and you appear strong, able to bear many sons."

Isabel's mouth dropped open. "No, Mrs. Stanfield. I'm only here as a companion for Susannah."

"You misunderstood, *mija.* He has promised me he'd search for a wife. He is a man of his word, a man of honor. He will court you, and you can be his wife as well as Susannah's companion. This will be best, *si?*"

"See?"

"It means yes in Spanish," Susannah whispered.

"Yes. I mean no. No! I will not marry your son. He doesn't

even like me. He wouldn't want me—I guarantee you that. And while I'm sure he's nice enough, he's not what I want, either. I mean—" What had she gotten herself into?

Isabel gazed helplessly to Susannah, who only shrugged her shoulders. "My mother is a very determined woman. She's afraid if Slade doesn't soon marry and produce heirs, our family will lose Rancho San Miguel. Besides, then you and I could be sisters, and you wouldn't have to leave, not ever."

Susannah's hopeful face made Isabel want to scream, "But I want to leave!" Slade hadn't mentioned anything about needing or desiring a wife. And truth be told, she wasn't exactly wifely. A companion for his lame sister was a difficult enough job for Isabel. Had she been brought here under false pretenses? Panic rose within, and she fought the urge to take flight.

"Why don't you show me to my room? I think I'd like to rid myself of this dress." The corset suddenly felt like it was cutting her in half. "May I borrow something less constraining?"

Susannah nodded.

"Excuse us, please, Mrs. Stanfield."

"*Si.* Supper will be ready shortly."

"Your room is the second door. Mine is the first," Susannah explained.

Once in her room, Isabel handed Susannah her cane.

Susannah moved toward the doorway. "I'll return shortly with a change of clothing."

Isabel removed the plaid suit coat, draping it across a chair in the corner. She unpinned the hat, wishing her red curls didn't insist on popping out every chance they got. She carefully set the hat on her bureau, letting her long, thick mane fall over her shoulders and back. Suddenly very tired from the trip and worried about the next six months, she laid across the bed, wishing she'd never come.

"Isabel, it's me." Her door swung open and Susannah appeared with an almost new outfit. "Look, I brought you split skirt, a bandana, and even a hat! Aren't they perfect?"

Perfect wouldn't have been the way Isabel chose to describe the wide-legged denim trousers that could almost pass for a skirt.

"You can ride in these. All the ranch women own a pair."

She couldn't disappoint Susannah. "As you said, these will be perfect." She took the offering.

"Meet me in the kitchen once you're dressed." Susannah closed the door behind her.

Isabel shed her long bodice and plaid skirt. She removed the slip, large bustle, and tight corset, and slipped into the blouse and culottes. Pulling the front of her hair up and pinning it in place, Isabel left the back long and free. Following the porch toward the west wing, she stopped short.

"Mother, I am not going to marry Isabel Fairchild!" Slade's voice carried to where Isabel quickly dashed behind a tall, treelike plant in one of the many clay pots. His mother must have approached him with her marriage nonsense, too.

"You promised, *mijo.*" Isabel noted the desperation in the woman's voice.

"I promised I'd consider the idea. I have and decided against it, but even if I changed my mind, Isabel Fairchild is not a candidate." Why did that bother her? He certainly was no candidate, either.

"She is pretty," Mrs. Stanfield insisted.

"She is tolerable, I suppose, but not tempting to me in the least. There is no beauty in her character, and should I ever marry, I must insist on a woman of strong character. Beautiful inside and out." Now his words stung, leaving Isabel's pride wounded.

"You must marry! What will happen to our land otherwise? My parents and grandparents worked hard for this *rancho*. You cannot throw that gift away by producing no heir. You gave your word."

Susannah was right—their mother was determined.

"Mother, I promised if and when Susannah is married, then and only then would I consider matrimony for myself."

Isabel heard Susannah shuffling toward her and knew she must come out of hiding before she got caught listening in on a conversation she wasn't part of. Lifting her chin, Isabel sauntered like a woman without a care in the world toward Slade and his mother.

❧

"You have not heard the end of this from me," his mother informed Slade on her way back into the kitchen.

He knew she'd not let it go, not as long as Isabel was here to remind her of his perceived need for a wife. And speaking of Isabel, Slade swallowed the interest he felt as she neared. She moved with grace, and her hair swung free and loose down her back. He rose. *Tolerable, but not tempting. What a liar I am. She nearly drives me out of my mind, she's so beautiful, but it wouldn't do to let Mother in on that secret. She'd have a preacher here so fast, I wouldn't know what hit me. And, honestly, I do doubt her character. What sort of woman of sensibility and integrity heads for Tombstone?*

He nodded toward Isabel. "Now you look more like a *ranchero*, senorita."

Isabel spun around, showing off the full effect of her new outfit. "And I'm fit for horseback riding."

"Oh, yes!"

At Susannah's voice, Isabel swung around; Susannah approached from behind her. "Riding a horse is—" Susannah stopped, looking like a girl who'd lost her best friend. "It was. . .was my favorite thing to do in the entire world."

Before the accident, Slade reminded himself.

"I don't know how to ride. I only spoke in jest," Isabel assured Susannah.

"Slade can teach you! He's a wonderful teacher and rider."

Slade planned to spend little to no time with Isabel, so Susannah's suggestion didn't sit well with him. "I have things to catch up on around here. No time for frivolous activity." He hated the disappointment his words brought to his sister's face. So much of her life these past three years had been disappointing.

"I thought September was a time for waiting." Isabel raised one brow in challenge, throwing his words back at him.

"The livestock and earth are waiting. The rancher is mending fences, painting barns, catching up on chores."

"I'll help you paint so you'll have more time to teach me to ride." She tilted her head and smiled a most pleasing smile, but her charm wouldn't sway him.

Spoiled and used to getting your own way, are you? "Miss Fairchild, may I remind you—your sole purpose here is Susannah, not riding or painting."

"Oh, Slade, please," Susannah begged. "I could sit and watch. It would bring me great pleasure. I haven't been to the barn since. . . Please, do it for me."

Susannah, however, could easily sway him. He knew he'd give in to her. "Fine." Isabel wore a satisfied smile when he turned to her. "Tomorrow will be your first lesson."

"Can we go to the barn this evening after dinner? I long for the smell of the horses and hay. I long to leave these walls," Susannah pleaded.

"Why haven't you gone to the barn?" Isabel asked Susannah

as they both sank into the chairs around the table where Slade sat.

Susannah glanced at him, and he fought the guilt assailing him. "It's for your own safety."

Isabel chewed her lip and frowned. "You force her to stay cooped up in the house?"

"It's for the best," Susannah assured her. "I know he's only protecting me."

"You haven't left this house since your accident?" Isabel's tone reflected both amazement and disapproval.

"This is family business," Slade informed her, not wanting this particular conversation to continue.

Isabel smiled, shaking her head. "And I'm not family, so you'd like me to keep quiet, wouldn't you, Mr. Stanfield?" The color rose in her cheeks and she stood. "Keeping her locked up here is inhuman. No wonder the poor girl is lonely and needs a companion. She is not an animal to be caged!"

Slade rose, equal to the confrontation. "Miss Fairchild, as I've already said, this matter is of no concern of yours. I do what is best for my sister."

Isabel's hands were balled into fists. "By bringing me here as her companion, you've made this my business! How can staying within ten feet of the house be best?"

Slade's voice rose. "It's safer!"

Isabel paced across the width of the porch and spun to face him. "The roof could fall on her head."

Mrs. Stanfield carried a plate of hot food from the kitchen. She placed it on the table. "She is right, Slade. You know the truth here." His mother laid her hand on his chest over his heart. "You can't control everything in Susannah's life—only God can."

Slade glimpsed Susannah's hopeful eyes. "Fine." He sighed.

"I'll take you and Miss Fairchild down to the barn after we finish supper." He settled back into his chair, and Isabel returned to hers. She might have won this battle, but she wouldn't win the war. Susannah lost one limb because he'd been careless with her; he wasn't about to let something worse happen if he could stop it.

Susannah reached over and squeezed his hand. "Thank you," she whispered just before her mother said grace. After the *amen,* she promised, "I'll be careful."

Slade determined to set Miss Fairchild straight after dinner. There'd be no more usurping his authority!

❧

Isabel decided they needed a change of topic to help break the tension. "Mrs. Stanfield, the meal is delicious." The spiced beef with cabbage had a unique flavor. "I think the beans are my favorite. I have never had anything like them."

"They are *frijoles* and so dear to my people's hearts. My grandmother taught me to cook them as a young girl."

"Mama mostly cooks the old recipes from Mexico," Susannah informed her. "And nobody cooks like her. She's teaching me. Maybe we can teach you, too."

"Maybe." Isabel peeked over at Slade. By the set of his jaw, she doubted she'd be here long enough to learn much of anything.

After dinner, Slade carried Susannah down near the barn; Isabel trailed behind. He lowered her to a bale of hay near a fenced riding area. "I'll be right back."

Susannah rotated and faced her. "This is where they break the wild colts and the very spot I learned to ride. At three, my papa brought me down here and placed me on my first pony."

"Well, well, well, hello there, Susannah, miss."

Isabel twisted and found one very handsome cowboy grinning at them. He removed his hat. "Name's Dusty, ma'am." He glowed golden from his sun-bronzed skin to his blond hair and light brown eyes. The admiration in his gaze renewed her confidence. This was the kind of attention she was used to.

Isabel returned his grin and was certain approval seeped from her eyes as well. "Hello there, Dusty. It's a great pleasure to meet you." Isabel extended her hand, which he cooperatively reached for and kissed. *Here is a man who knows how to treat a lady, unlike Slade Stanfield.* "I'm Isabel Fairchild."

"Well, Miss Isabel Fairchild, I assure you the pleasure is all mine." He bowed from the waist, still holding her hand. "And Miss Susannah, how good to see you. I've missed you."

"Dusty, I believe there is work to be done—work you're being paid to do." Slade walked toward them, leading a horse, a disapproving scowl plastered on his face.

four

"I'm done for the night, Mr. Stanfield." Dusty placed his hat on his head and sent an amused expression in Isabel's direction. He waltzed over and settled on the hay next to Susannah. "Think I'll just sit here a spell and keep Miss Susannah company." He all but dared Slade to make him leave.

Slade gritted his teeth. "Are you going to ride or stand there?" he snapped at Isabel.

"Ride, of course." She grinned and moved to the horse. Slade liked being in control of all things, and Dusty's appearance had ruffled his plan. Roughly, Slade lifted her into the saddle. He led the horse to the arena. She waited until Dusty and Susannah were out of earshot. "Another bond servant?"

He glared up at her. "He tends to be lazy."

"And that gives you the right to be rude?"

"I wasn't rude. I'm growing tired of insolent employees usurping my authority." Isabel knew he had directed the remark at her. "And," he continued, "I'd appreciate you keeping your opinions regarding my sister to yourself."

"I may not be able to do that," Isabel answered honestly.

"Then I may not be able to keep you here for six months." Slade stopped the horse on the other side of the ring and faced her.

"You are a dictator and a bully, aren't you?"

"If I have to be. Now do you want to ride this mare or not?"

Oh, the man infuriated her. She wanted to stomp her foot and yell but was afraid of scaring the horse. "Yes."

Slade went through the paces of teaching her to stop, go, and turn in both directions. All the while, he kept a close eye on Dusty and Susannah. Their chatter and laughter seemed only to goad him into a worse mood. After Isabel practiced each command several times, Slade had her ride to the gate; he lifted her down before opening it.

Isabel looked at the horse for the first time. She had kind eyes, unlike her owner.

"Slade, she's a beautiful little mare. When did you get her?" Susannah asked. Dusty had assisted her in walking to where they stood; she clung to his arm.

"Don't let her size fool you," Dusty said. He lifted Susannah into the saddle recently vacated by Isabel. "She's small but a powerful runner."

Susannah patted the dapple-gray neck. Pure pleasure radiated from her face.

Isabel peeked at Slade; he appeared near the boiling point. "What's her name?" Isabel asked, rubbing the velvet-soft nose.

"Lady," Dusty answered

"It suits her," Susannah proclaimed.

"She should be running in that race two months from now." Dusty absently stroked her head.

"What race?" both Isabel and Susannah asked simultaneously.

"Enough chatter. It's time to rub this mare down and put her away." Slade unceremoniously pulled Susannah off the horse and plopped her back on the bale of hay. Then grabbing the reins from Dusty, he led the mare toward the barn.

The three of them stared after him. "I'm so sorry. I don't know what's gotten into my brother. He's never rude."

Never rude? That was news to Isabel.

Susannah now stood, holding on to the fence for support. "Please, Dusty, tell us about this race."

"Oh, you know, the annual event at the Ochoa ranch." Dusty walked over and brought Susannah closer to him and Isabel.

Susannah let out a sigh filled with longing. "I have missed that! Isabel you must go. Perhaps Dusty might escort you."

Susannah glanced at Dusty, and Isabel glanced at the barn, knowing full well Slade would forbid her attending. "What is the Ochoa ranch and this race? Tell me about it." Sounded like an adventure, indeed.

"All the ranchers from around the area gather at the Ochoas' place for a picnic and horse racing." Dusty dug the toe of his boot into the ground. "Wish Slade would let me race Lady. On a short sprint, I don't think a horse in southern California could beat her."

"I remember those days at the Ochoas'. We'd get up before dawn to get an early start. I could hardly sleep the night before. Oh, Isabel, there were so many people, so much excitement. There'd be dancing and singing, horse races and buggy races." Susannah's face lit with her memories. "I wish Slade wasn't so determined to protect me from all of life."

An idea formed. "Dusty, if I can secure Mrs. Stanfield's approval, would you chaperone the three of us to this big event?"

A momentary fear crossed his face. "I don't know, Miss Fairchild. Mr. Stanfield might have my hide for that."

Isabel tilted her head to the right, just so, batted her eyes in a pleading manner, and laid her hand on his arm. "Why I'd be so obliged, I'd dance every dance with only you." Isabel watched the inner war Dusty fought play out across his face. The promise of dancing every dance with him worked in her favor. He wanted to say yes, but she knew he feared risking the fury of Mr. Stanfield.

"I need this job, ma'am."

Isabel raised her brows—one step ahead of Dusty in working

this out to everyone's advantage, everyone, that is, except Slade Stanfield. "Perhaps Mrs. Stanfield will order you to take us. There won't be a thing he can do about that, now will there?"

"Isabel, I don't want to hurt or upset Slade. He's a dear brother and always has my best first and foremost in his mind."

"Well then, he'll be agreeable if you need a change of scene, some fresh air, and sunshine, now won't he?"

"I'm not sure my mother would go against Slade's wishes." Susannah's forehead creased in worry.

Isabel patted her hand. "I think she made her feelings clear earlier at supper. She doesn't believe Slade has the right to keep you prisoner in your own home, either."

Isabel watched Slade walk toward them from the barn. His bowed legs testified to his life on the range. He wore his hat pulled low on his brow, making his eyes shadowed. Why was he such a stubborn man when it came to his sister? Didn't he know bad things could happen anywhere, even inside the house?

Isabel whispered, "Let's say nothing more until I speak to your mother. I will honor whatever she says." *But I may use a little persuasion first.*

Susannah nodded, and all three looked toward Slade. His brooding presence cast a gloom on their conversation. "Ladies, it's time to return to the house." He swept Susannah into his arms and dismissed Dusty with a look.

Isabel lagged behind. "I promise I'll do nothing that might risk your good standing here at the ranch," she whispered. "It was very good to meet you, Mr. . ." Isabel spoke loudly for Slade's benefit.

"Mr. Thomas."

She smiled and nodded. "Lovely to meet you, Mr. Thomas." To ensure his future loyalty, she stood on tiptoe and kissed his cheek.

Slade had stopped and was waiting for her. He shot daggers at her with his gaze. She hadn't intended for him to see the kiss, but he had. His wrath was all too evident. She even spotted disappointment in Susannah's eyes.

Oh, well. Isabel tossed her hair and walked right past them. For the first time in her life, she'd found a purpose, something more important than herself. Susannah—kind, loving Susannah—needed her to break down the prison walls Slade had so carefully erected. And while Isabel was on this ranch, she'd spend all her time and energy finding ways to do just that.

She entered the house through the front door, holding it open for Slade and Susannah. "I'm exhausted. If you'll both excuse me, I shall retire to my room. Good night." She marched straight to her room. Tomorrow morning, she'd help Mrs. Stanfield with breakfast, and they'd have a talk about that son of hers.

❧

Slade couldn't get out of his mind the picture of Isabel kissing Dusty weeks ago. The woman had been here only a couple of months and had caused more trouble than a loose bull with a bee on his back. Why did it bother him so much? He liked her less each day, so why did he care? Susannah. She must be the reason. After all, she looked up to Isabel, and he didn't want her copying Isabel's unladylike behavior.

They'd learned to avoid each other well, though. He'd changed his habits, making sure Isabel was finished with her breakfast before he came in from his chores to have his. They saw each other only on Sundays when the family went to church and at dinner, and that was a quiet affair. When he walked into a room, everyone seemed to choose silence.

He came through the back of the house and into the kitchen. "Morning, Mama." He kissed her cheek.

"Morning, Slade." She handed him a plate of ham and eggs, which he carried to the porch. She brought out a pan of warm biscuits and took the chair across from his. He knew immediately they were about to embark on a serious conversation by the determined set of her jaw.

"Next week is the annual Ochoa party."

Slade laid his fork down, dreading her next words.

"Dusty will escort Susannah, Isabel, and myself, unless you'd like the honor."

"How did that woman talk you into this?" He rose from his chair, scraping it across the tile. "You know how I feel about keeping Susannah safe." He ran a hand through his hair.

"Please sit down, Slade, and we will discuss this without anger."

He honored his mother's wishes and returned to his seat. "How can you expect me not to be angry? She went behind my back."

"Going to you would be hopeless, would it not?" His mother had that knowing glint in her eye.

He nodded.

"Slade, it is time. Susannah is a vibrant young woman. You cannot keep her locked away forever. I allowed it for a while, thinking it would help you cope, but it hasn't. You must forgive yourself; Susannah has. Why can't you?"

Slade didn't know the answer. All he knew was his sister—his dearly loved sister—had lost her leg due to his careless behavior. How could a man forgive himself for such an offense? He couldn't, but at least he'd stay nearby and try to prevent anything else from harming her. Pushing his barely eaten breakfast away, he stood and returned his hat to his head. "I'll take you."

His mother nodded, sadness in her eyes. He hated knowing he was the reason.

"I'm going to get back to work. I'll see you at noon."

Fuming, he decided to hunt down Isabel and give her a piece of his mind, but he found Susannah instead, snuggled in a comfortable chair with her Bible. "Where is Isabel?"

"While I do my study, she enjoys a morning walk." Susannah closed her Bible and laid it in her lap. "Mama told you, didn't she?"

"Yes, and I will be there with you." He removed his hat again and twirled it on his finger.

"Please don't be angry. I so appreciate all you do for me." Susannah smiled, but in her eyes resided the same sorrow he'd seen in his mother's. "You are the best brother a girl could ask for, and I'm glad you'll be attending the party with us. Oh, Slade, I do so miss things such as this. Please understand, if you keep me locked in this house too much longer, I shall simply go crazy."

"And please understand, Susannah, if anything else happened to you, I could not live with myself." He gripped his hat so tight the brim crumpled.

"God is in control. What He allows in our lives, we must accept as His will."

"How can it be His will for a beautiful, young girl to lose a leg? Was it also His will that her brother behave in a careless manner?"

"Slade, we were just having fun. I in no way hold you responsible. I've assured you of this countless times. God could have prevented my leg from being crushed, but He allowed it. He has His reasons. I know not what they are, but I trust Him implicitly. He loves me and has my best in mind."

"But I was responsible, and I'm not nearly as charitable as you, my dear sister."

Susannah's expression bore resignation. "I pray you will

learn to be charitable to yourself and to all people I love, even Isabel."

Slade scoffed.

"I fear that will never happen." Isabel's voice came from behind him.

"Miss Fairchild, you are just the person I wished to see."

"That surprises me." He'd come to expect her frankness.

"May I speak to you alone?" He held his temper in check, not wanting Susannah to witness his ire.

"If you must." Isabel glanced in Susannah's direction.

Susannah smiled her encouragement, then turned her gaze to Slade. "Remember the charity we just spoke of?" she whispered. "Now might be a good time to employ it."

Slade had no intention of being charitable to Miss Fairchild. She deserved no such treatment. She'd come uninvited into his life and turned his world upside down. Now he would give her the verbal lashing she so deserved, but if his wrath frightened her, she hid it well.

Slade held the door for Isabel. "Have you walked down to the river yet?"

"No, not yet."

He set off in an easterly direction. "I'm surprised, given your propensity toward adventure. Of course it's ill advised for a young woman to walk to the river alone, but that would certainly be all the more reason for you to insist on doing it. Would it not?"

"Why don't you speak what's on your mind, Mr. Stanfield, instead of playing word games filled with sarcasm."

He'd planned to wait until they were well away from the house and barn before they started their verbal sparring. "You know good and well what's on my mind."

"The warm air smells of mountain lilac and wild mustard.

How can you walk through this beautiful valley and not be infatuated with all you see and smell and hear?"

Her question caught Slade completely unaware.

Isabel spun around, arms extended wide, eyes raised to the sky. "How can you breathe in all the smells of this ranch and not want Susannah to have the same privilege? How can you not see the hills and want her to climb them? See the horses and not want her to ride them? See the river and not want her to swim?"

Isabel stopped and looked deep into his soul. Tears brimmed in her eyes. "Susannah sings your praises and believes you to be the most wonderful man on the face of the earth, but I believe you to be the most selfish." She resumed her walk toward the river.

Slade grabbed her arm; she stopped and faced him. With her jaw clenched, she was ready for a fight.

"Do you see my barn over there?"

Isabel nodded, clearly confused by his response.

"That barn isn't big enough to hold all the guilt I have over Susannah, so I don't need your help making me feel worse. And I don't need you reminding me of all the things she can't do, all the things in life she's missing out on." Slade swallowed, hoping to loosen the lump growing in his throat.

Isabel pulled her arm from his grip and rubbed the spot where his hand had been. "Slade, I'm not trying to make you feel worse—only to help you see the possibilities. I want you to permit me to open up the world to her, and I want you to quit being so ridiculous and overprotective. You haven't allowed her to live since the accident. She merely exists locked away in that house all the time." The passion in her eyes testified to how strongly Isabel felt about Susannah's having a chance for normalcy, but she didn't understand. *Maybe it's me who refuses to understand.*

Slade rubbed the back of his neck and sighed. "Do you know how Susannah lost her leg?"

Isabel shook her head.

He began to walk again, not wanting her peering into his face as he tried to make her see reason. "I was responsible. We entered the buggy race at the Ochoas'. I hated losing, and we were in second. I took the turn too fast because I wanted the prize." He kept his face turned from her, not wanting to see pity in her eyes.

"Even so, Susannah has no bitterness regarding the accident. She told me she grieved, accepted it, and now she'd like to move on. When will you let that happen? When will you accept it and move on?"

"I was reckless, and now my sister can't walk, let alone climb hills." He looked around at all the hills they'd once climbed together as children. His heart clenched at the reality. "How does someone forgive himself for such an atrocity?"

Isabel stopped, and he followed suit, though he didn't turn face her. He kept his eyes on the brown and yellow earth beneath his feet.

"I don't know, Slade. I don't know." She laid a hand on his arm. "I only know locking her away isn't the answer." Her hushed tone carried compassion and tenderness.

"I don't want anything to hurt her, not ever again."

"Neither do I. Neither does your mother." Isabel moved around in front of him and took hold of his hands. "But none of us has that sort of control over another's life. People we love get hurt. I don't know why, but I've lived long enough to know it is so."

All his anger had faded, and what Isabel said almost made sense. His well-meaning plan to keep Susannah safe and to control her environment was being blown to bits by one determined, fiery-haired woman. He made the mistake of looking up into those green eyes, and he forgot how much he disliked her, forgot how headstrong she was, and forgot everything except her lips. Those he couldn't forget, and he inched his way toward them.

five

Isabel's heart pounded so hard, she no longer even heard the rushing of the river. *Slade's going to kiss me.* Shocked both by the fact that he would and how much she wanted him to, she anticipated their lips meeting. When he laid his palm against her cheek, she closed her eyes. His kiss—long, slow, and so very wonderful—was like none other. It wasn't playful, or pretend, or just for fun.

When it ended, he rested his forehead against hers. One hand still held hers and the other lay against her cheek. He traced her lips with his thumb. "Isabel," he whispered.

She saw remorse in his eyes. "Please, no regrets." Feeling vulnerable, she twisted away from him, wrapping her arms around her waist. "It was, after all, just a kiss. No obligations, no expectations," she said, pretending it was so. For some reason the kiss mattered very much to her, but she'd not let him know that. "I've been kissed by at least a dozen boys."

"Have you ever been kissed by a man, Isabel?" His tone was thick and husky. He pulled her back into his arms, wrapping her in his embrace and sliding his hand through her hair. Gently his lips met hers. *No, I've never been kissed by a man before, not until now.* He settled that question once and for all time. His was the kiss of a man, and she kissed him back with the kiss of a woman.

She'd not let him know how deeply he affected her. Lightly, she said, "I think not, but if you'd like to practice, I have no objection to helping you learn. You, Mr. Stanfield, might one day learn to kiss like a man."

He laughed, shaking his head and lingering there holding her, burying his face in her hair. Isabel laid her cheek against his chest, feeling content for the first time in a very long while. She loved the steady beat of his heart and the deep roots he had in this land. She loved the way he cared for his mother and sister, even if he went about it utterly and completely wrong. She loved being here on this ranch and investing in Susannah's life. She loved kissing him, and if doing so would make her stay more delightsome, then so be it.

The thought of kissing this man often seemed pleasing, indeed. Just to prove it, she pulled his head toward her for another try. Their third kiss was short and lighthearted, but nonetheless sweet.

He released her and took her hand. They followed the river for a ways, both obviously contemplating the tenderness they'd shared. He'd surprised her and shown a vulnerable side. Her heart surprised her with all the new feelings churning inside. *How can I help him and Susannah both? They need me.* No one had ever needed Isabel, and it was certainly a grand feeling.

Too soon he dropped her hand, and Isabel sensed his distress over their kisses. *"She is tolerable, I suppose, but not tempting to me in the least."* His words to his mother returned to her. No wonder he felt remorse. *"There is no beauty in her character."* He didn't even like her. *"I must insist on a woman of strong character. Beautiful inside and out."* Nor did he consider her pretty—inside or out.

Isabel watched a hummingbird whiz around the wild tobacco blossoms, wondering how she could handle this ordeal with the least embarrassment. She couldn't bear his rejection. A woodpecker hammered a tree trunk, and she understood his frustration. Reaching Slade's heart would prove as impossible as making a hole in a tree with her head.

The worst part was that this really hurt. He mattered to her. His opinion mattered.

❧

Slade had known his attraction to Isabel was strong, but what had he done? Kissing her, touching her, holding her only made his plight twice as difficult. His life was no longer his own; he'd devoted it to Susannah's well-being. How could he fall in love when Susannah never would? Every possible suitor fled after she'd been injured. Apparently, no man wanted a wife with a wooden leg. It was because of his carelessness that she'd be a spinster. He could not allow himself to have what she never would.

"Slade." Isabel's voice broke into his thoughts.

"Umm?" he asked absentmindedly, still brooding over his dilemma.

"I fear I've given you the wrong impression." She stopped and turned to face him. "I'm not interested in you as a beau." Isabel was nothing if not frank.

"I see." Though he knew this was for the best, disappointment settled in his heart.

"I did, however, enjoy the kisses." Pleasure filled her face. "Though they still need some work," she teased. "Sadly though, I won't be able to help you in that capacity."

"You won't?" More disappointment instead of relief.

"You see, I find myself quite fond of Dusty."

"Dusty?" The man's name brought a pang of jealousy.

"So for me to accept your affection would be most inappropriate. Would you not agree?"

They had arrived back at the barn. He paused at the door. "Yes, most inappropriate." Slade tipped his hat. "I'll be sure and act in a more gentlemanly manner in the future. Good day, Miss Fairchild."

Slade was now over an hour behind on his work. He grabbed the pitchfork. *Dusty!*

Wait! Maybe Dusty was the solution to all Slade's problems. Isabel wasn't ready to settle down and get serious with anyone, so if he could convince Dusty to spend a little brotherly time with her, she'd be occupied and less likely to wreak havoc on Slade's own emotions. Sure, Dusty was his answer. Slade saddled up and searched for his foreman. He found him in the north field, running new fence line.

"I need a little help from you." Slade swung down off his saddle.

"Sure, boss. What's up?" Dusty straightened and gave his crew the sign to take a five-minute break.

"I'd like you to court Miss Fairchild."

Dusty raised his brows. "Miss Fairchild?"

"You can help me keep an eye on her, keep her in line, and keep my mother from pestering me as well."

"In line?"

"She's a wild one that Isabel. I don't want that sort of influence rubbing off on Susannah. I thought having a beau might tame her some."

"You want me to be Miss Fairchild's beau?" Dusty shook his head. "I don't know, Mr. Stanfield. That doesn't seem too honest."

Dusty's words pricked Slade's conscience; he, however, ignored the jab.

"You'll be spending a little time in the company of one mighty pretty woman. Maybe you'll decide you like her; maybe you won't."

"And what's this about your mother?"

"She has some idea Isabel would be a good wife for me."

Dusty cocked his head. "As you said, she's one pretty lady.

You could do worse."

Slade lost his patience. "Will you or not?" he demanded.

"What about Miss Susannah? Isn't Miss Fairchild her companion?"

"Take her along."

Dusty's face lit up. "Two pretty ladies I can handle." He shook Slade's hand. "You've got yourself a deal there, boss."

❧

Trudging from the barn toward the house, Isabel didn't feel as relieved as she'd hoped. Truthfully, she felt downright deceitful. Why had she deceived Slade? She shook her head, disgusted with herself. *Only to save face and spare my pride.* Somehow, she'd convinced herself that rejecting him before he could reject her was the best thing to do. Now she felt ashamed.

"Isabel, is everything satisfactory?" Susannah waited for her on the front veranda, her voice anxious.

"Fine." Isabel forced a smile and swallowed, hoping to dislodge her displeasure with herself.

"Come sit with me." Susannah patted the wooden bench next to where she sat. "Did Slade say something to upset you?"

Isabel stared at the hands in her lap. "No. He was the perfect. . ." *Kisser?* "Gentleman." She didn't want to be interviewed by Susannah just now. Much too vulnerable, she might let her feelings slip. Taking a deep breath, Isabel jumped to her feet. "I'm certain we need some fresh air and sunshine. A walk will lift my glum and brighten your pale face."

"But Slade won't allow that." Susannah pulled herself to a stand, leaning on her cane.

"He and I had a talk—" But she couldn't remember exactly how the discussion ended. Untrue, she did remember exactly how it ended—with a few heart-stopping kisses. But she couldn't remember the decision they'd reached. "Anyway, he didn't dispute the fact that you, my dear, need a life." Isabel smiled. "So today your life shall begin!"

"Oh, Isabel, thank you."

Isabel took the cane in her left hand and extended her right for Susannah.

"Walking with me, you might not go far," Susannah warned as they crossed the porch.

"How far doesn't matter. Just enjoy the day."

"I will. Let's walk toward the pond. It was always my favorite place."

"The pond it shall be."

"Isabel, tell me about you. Why are you going to Arizona? Why do you never speak of your family? Are you running from something?"

Moving over the dead stubble of grass at a snail's pace, Isabel took her time forming her answer. Slade had warned her not to shock Susannah with the truth of who she was, but there was enough pretense between her and Slade; she'd not deceive Susannah, too. "Not from something, but hopefully to something."

"What do you mean?"

"I'm the youngest of three girls—"

"You have sisters! I've always wished for sisters." Susannah's exuberance made Isabel smile.

"And I have always wished for a brother."

"Mine is truly wonderful, but it's still not the same. We can't giggle together and share clothes."

Isabel laughed. "No, Slade would look pretty silly in this split skirt you loaned me."

"And he has no interest in hair or embroidery."

Isabel crinkled her nose. "I confess, embroidery bores me to tears."

Susannah giggled. "What do you enjoy, Isabel?"

"Sewing. I've made my sisters several dresses. I love hair and fashion. I've tried drawing but am not very good. I wished to be musical, but that talent escaped me as well. The awful truth is there isn't much I'm very good at."

"That cannot be true."

"I feel certain your brother would agree. I enjoy the frivolities of life—parties, dancing, the theater. I'm not much good on a place like this." Isabel spread her shawl near the edge of the pond and helped Susannah lower herself onto it.

Susannah took Isabel's hand. "You've been good for me. I'm quite indebted. I haven't seen this pond in three years. Do you know what a gift you've given me? And as for Slade, I wish you could have known him before—" She let go of Isabel's hand and pointed to her leg. "Before this." Susannah smiled, remembering. "He was so much like you, Isabel, filled with laughter and merriment. So alive, so jovial. There was nothing we didn't try at least once, much to Mama's chagrin."

Isabel imagined Slade enjoying life instead of brooding. "I would very much have liked knowing that Slade." *I already very much like knowing this one.* Though she ached for him. "If only he could forgive himself."

"I pray for that every day." Susannah untied her shoe and kicked it off.

"My father has a strong faith like yours. I've never really understood." Isabel followed Susannah's lead, ridding herself of shoes and stockings as well. "When I was ten, his bank closed down, and he sold our beautiful mansion to help return some of the depositors' money. He bought a small cottage for the family and became a fisherman. His main reason was to get me and my two sisters away from the influences of society and give us a simpler and more God-focused upbringing.

He'd surrendered his life to God a couple of years before all that happened. He changed so much and wanted each of us to change as well."

"He sounds like a man of integrity."

Isabel nodded, and a wave of longing washed over her. How she'd love to see her family again. The desire caught her by surprise.

"Will you help me up? I cannot be this close to that water and not wade in, letting my foot enjoy the cool wetness."

Isabel jumped up and pulled Susannah to her feet. They shuffled to the water's edge. Isabel curled her toes in the damp sand. She pulled her riding skirt up to her knees. Susannah lifted her skirt and tied it up, exposing part of her thigh. They both laughed.

"Good thing there are no men around."

Isabel waited until Susannah had a firm hold on her. Then they waded out until the water circled their knees. Susannah had much difficulty between the water, the sand, and her wooden leg. Finally, she gave up and fell forward into the pond, catching herself with her hands. She splashed Isabel. "Swimming will be much easier than trudging through all this."

Isabel splashed her back, waded farther out, and dove in. She swam out toward the center. The pond was chilly but a pleasant relief from the heat of the day. Isabel was surprised by the cold San Diego mornings and the dry, hot afternoons. She shook the water from her face and found Susannah right next to her.

"Is it safe for you to be out this far?"

"As safe as it is for you." Susannah's face shone. "Swimming is easier than walking."

They swam together back to the shore. Both laid on their

backs in the shallow water, staring up at the sky. "You still never told me about your family. We got as far as two sisters."

"Gabrielle and Magdalene."

"Tell me about them."

"Magdalene and her husband, Chandler, run an orphanage. I once fancied myself in love with him, but he chose Magdalene—sweet, plain, God-fearing Magdalene." *Everything I'm not.* "Gabrielle is married to a fisherman. Slade would like her because she *is* beautiful inside and out."

"Why do you say Slade would like her?" Susannah grabbed her arm. "Are we moving?"

"I think we are. Let's just lie here and float for a while. Hang on to me, and we'll swim back when we grow tired."

"Now back to Slade."

Isabel hoped Susannah would forget, but she hadn't. "I just heard him comment to your mother once that the only kind of woman he'd be interested in was one of character—beautiful inside and out. Gabrielle is."

"So are you, Isabel." Susannah spoke softly, barely above the splashing of the waves.

"My parents don't think so. I disappoint them often with my choices, so I have given up." Isabel felt the pain their displeasure always brought.

"Is that why you left?"

"That and the fact my father arranged a marriage for me." Isabel paused, remembering. "I don't want you to think badly of them. My parents are good people, but they don't understand me, nor I them. It felt like I never measured up to the person they hoped I'd be. Never measured up to the people my sisters are. The type of person my parents and Slade would admire."

"Do you want him to admire you?"

Isabel swatted at a mosquito. "Doesn't everyone enjoy being well thought of?"

"I suppose they do. You know, Isabel, Mama's right. You'd be a perfect wife for Slade."

Isabel smiled. *Slade would be perfect for me.* "I have grand plans, Susannah, and they don't include a husband. Besides, I just confessed to you how useless I'd be on a place like this."

"These grand plans, what do they include?"

❧

"Susannah! Isabel!" Slade yelled at the top of his voice. Both startled and swam toward shore.

"What were they doing out there floating all the way on the other side of the pond?" he asked his mother.

"Enjoying life. Something you never do anymore," she responded.

"Hiring her was the biggest mistake of my life." Slade paced the shoreline. "She's too adventuresome, too much like I used to be. She'll end up getting Susannah killed."

His mother grabbed his arm, forcing him to stop and look into her eyes. "Would you rather her die a prisoner, *Mijo?*"

"Neither," he snapped. "I'm firing Miss Fairchild. She can earn her passage to Arizona somewhere else."

His mother dropped his arm. "You can't fire her for being determined to give your sister a second chance at life."

"No, but I can fire her for disobeying a direct order." Hands on his hips, he waited at the water's edge.

"A direct order? Is this the military?"

"Why are they swimming so slowly?" Slade unbuttoned his outer shirt.

"I'm sure they are resting for a moment. Susannah's had no exertion in three years. Her endurance must be low."

He handed his mother his shirt.

"What are you doing?"

"Getting ready to save one or both of them," he informed her, removing his boots.

"Slade, they'll get back to shore just fine without you, and you are not firing Isabel."

He faced his mother, clenching his fists. "She can't grasp the reality of Susannah's limitations. A young woman with a missing leg can't live a normal life! Am I the only person to understand this fact?"

"Slade, the only thing preventing me from living a normal life is you!"

Slade spun to face the pond. His heart broke watching his once virile sister crawling through the mud, unable to walk from the pond on two legs. He lifted her wet, soggy body from the ground and held her close. "Are you crying?"

"Yes."

Slade caught a glimpse of Mama and Miss Fairchild out of the corner of his eye. They walked together toward the house, both solemn with their heads hanging down. "Were you afraid? Is that why you're crying?"

Susannah punched his chest—hard—with her right hand while clinging to him with her left. "I can't do this anymore. I can't remain locked up. You have to let me have a life!" She fell into him, sobbing, and if he hadn't already been wet from holding her, she'd have soaked him with her tears.

He held Susannah and let her cry, feeling angrier than ever with Isabel. He resented her interference, resented his attraction to her, but most of all, he resented the rift she'd caused between him and Susannah. They never argued, and she'd not been angry with him for years, not until today.

"Susannah—"

"Don't say it, Slade. Do not tell me this is for my best!" She raised her head and lifted her gaze to his. "This is for *your* best, not mine. You want to keep me locked away safe and sound, so you don't worry. You have no regard for me or my needs."

Her teary eyes and accusations stabbed his heart with grief. Isabel must have put those ideas in her head. He remembered her words from this morning. *Susannah sings your praises and believes you to be the most wonderful man on the face of the earth, but I believe you to be the most selfish.*

"Until recently—until Isabel filled your mind with her thoughts—you were content." Slade carried Susannah to a nearby log. He retrieved her shoe, then sat down next to her.

"Resigned, not content. There is a world of difference." Her expression pleaded for understanding. "I can't go back." She crossed her arms in determined fashion. "Now that I've been away from the house, I cannot return to the confinement you wish me to live in. I cannot."

Slade rose from the log and paced a few feet away. Facing her, he said, "Now I fear I must resign myself to yours and Isabel's escapades. Isabel's stubborn refusal to submit to my authority as her boss has rubbed off on you and Mother. I have no alternative but to grudgingly give you your way."

A huge smile curved Susannah's lips. "Please don't be mad. I promise to be careful."

"Promise me you'll never leave the house again without Mother knowing the exact direction you shall take."

"I promise. Thank you, Slade. Thank you."

He lifted Susannah and carried her home. He had not the patience to spend the time needed for her to walk. When they arrived, he deposited her in her room for a change of clothes.

He knocked on Miss Fairchild's door. This was the second time in one day he'd searched her out for a talking-to, only this one wouldn't end with a kiss. He'd guarantee that.

Isabel swung her door open. Her hair was down, still damp and curling wildly. He swallowed and looked away, staring at some spot beyond her. For some reason, her hair and eyes intrigued him most.

"May we talk?"

"Two summons in one day?" Isabel raised a brow and followed him to the front porch. He motioned for her to sit on the wooden bench.

"If it were my decision alone, you'd be packing your bag to leave at this very moment, but, for some reason unknown to me, my mother and sister insist on your continuing here."

Isabel bit her bottom lip, and he knew she fought her frank nature.

"If you ever leave this house with my sister again and don't let my mother know exactly where you'll be, I will put you on the next train, no matter how much they disagree. Do you understand?"

"Tell me, Slade, what bothers you the most—that I enjoy life or that you've forgotten how? I'm very sorry. I never intended to frighten you or your mother. Now if you'll excuse me, I promised to help in the kitchen."

What bothered him most? Just about everything about Isabel bothered him.

six

The day of the races came, and Isabel climbed out of bed before sunrise. She heard Susannah's peg leg against the floor and knew she was up as well. Isabel braided her hair and carefully dressed in a real cowgirl outfit. It was the first time she'd worn honest-to-goodness men's trousers, chaps, a shirt, and vest. She tied a bandana around her neck and slid a hat low on her brow just the way Slade did. For the finishing touch, she pulled her braids forward so they hung down in the front.

Looking in the mirror, she smiled at the final result, pleased with her new appearance. *What will Slade think?* Why did she waste so much time contemplating him and wishing? She hadn't seen him since the pond incident and knew he intentionally avoided her. The friendship with his mother and sister continued, and she was growing to love them both. If only she and Slade could find some neutral territory on which to build a friendship.

She blew out her lamp and grabbed the Levi jacket Susannah had loaned her. Stopping by Susannah's room, she offered her an arm out to the buckboard. As they walked across the porch, she realized how much she'd grown to love this place—the house, the ranch, her and Susannah's daily visit to the pond. She had four months left to enjoy it, but she feared upon leaving, she'd miss this place and the people very much. Even Slade. Mostly Slade.

He lifted his mother, then Susannah, and then Isabel into the back of the wagon. His large hands spanning her waist was enough to give her heart a jolt. He didn't comment on how she looked, but his eyes seemed pleased nonetheless. She smiled at him, and he gave her a tiny nod to acknowledge he'd noticed.

"I filled the back of the wagon with straw to make your ride more comfortable," Slade stated to no one in particular.

"Good morning, ladies." Dusty rode up on Lady, grinning. "Slade's going to let me race her in the quarter mile today." He dismounted and tied the mare to the back of the wagon, hopping up on the seat next to Slade.

Slade signaled the team and the wagon jerked forward.

"We're off!" Susannah could barely contain her excitement.

"Isabel, this day is a custom passed down from the time my grandfather and his best friend, Jose Ochoa, got land grants from the Mexican government for two parcels of land beside each other." Mrs. Stanfield's eyes lit up as she remembered. "It comes from old Spanish times in California when the ranch owners invited the whole countryside to come and feast. It has been a great and wonderful event in my family since before my birth. You won't find anything like it in the whole world, except here in California."

Isabel enjoyed hearing Mrs. Stanfield reminisce while Slade drove the wagon over the sun-browned hills to the next valley. The Ochoa ranch had whitewashed fences and large, rolling pastures filled with mares and yearlings. They were nearly the first to arrive since they lived the closest, but several families were there who had come the night before.

Slade parked the buckboard and unhitched the horses while Dusty retrieved Lady and led her to a grassy spot under a shady tree and tied her there. He removed her saddle and patted her on the rump before leaving her. He lifted both Stanfield women from the wagon first, commenting on how beautiful each looked on this wonderful autumn day.

"Miss Fairchild." He reached for her, but his hands around her didn't affect her the way Slade's nearness did.

"Would you take a walk with me?" she asked.

He shrugged. "Sure." He held out his arm and she threaded hers through his.

Isabel licked her lips, feeling guilty about her plan. "I wondered if you and I could pretend to. . .well, sort of be courting?" She felt her face grow hot at the request.

Dusty stopped and faced Isabel. "What are you up to now?"

"Now?"

"Well, didn't you scheme your way into getting the whole family here today? Not that I don't appreciate it." He smiled and tapped the end of her nose with his forefinger.

Scheme? He made her sound conniving and underhanded. *Well, isn't that just what I am?* Isabel let out a long, slow breath. "Now I'm up to convincing Mrs. Stanfield and Susannah that I'm not the right girl for Slade."

He chuckled and raised a brow. "You and Slade?"

Why was the idea so funny? "Yes, me and Slade," Isabel snapped. "Will you help me or not?"

"Sure." He tucked her hand in the crook of his arm and led her down to admire the yearlings and two year olds. "Slade is watching us. Is that what you want?"

Isabel sighed again and leaned on the fence, admiring all the beautiful colts prancing around. They seemed to sense the excitement of the day. "I don't know. I suppose."

Dusty eyed her with frank appraisal. "Are you trying to convince the Stanfield women you're the wrong girl or convince Slade you're the right girl by making him jealous?"

"Maybe a little of both," Isabel confessed.

"You like him?" Dusty clearly wondered why.

"Sometimes, but he has no interest in me."

"None? I find that hard to believe. You're a beautiful woman, Isabel."

She grinned at his compliment. "Slade doesn't think so. I overheard him telling his mother as much. I've tried flirting and pouring on the charm, but he remains distant and unmoved."

Dusty frowned. "Isabel, what intrigues you—the man or the conquest?"

She raised her eyes heavenward. "Frankly, both. He's the first man I couldn't interest, even for a brief period of time. I guess my pride is hurt. And he needs me."

"How so?"

"He needs to learn to relax and have fun. I'm just the girl to teach him."

"Maybe he's more interested than you think. He can't seem to quit watching us."

"Probably just grateful I'm not bothering him."

"I don't know. He's a pretty complicated character. He's so serious, and you're so carefree. You two are like oil and water. Are you sure he's what you want?" Dusty placed a boot toe up on the fence.

"Not forever, but while I'm here. He's constant, stable, unchanging." She rattled off his attributes that drew her to him.

"Unbending?"

"That, too, but maybe I can teach him to live again." A colt meandered over to them, and Isabel scratched the gray foal behind the ears. "How long have you known him?"

"I've worked at the ranch four years. Why?" A bay strode up to them and Dusty stroked its neck.

"So you knew him before?"

"The accident? Yes. He was a different man back then."

"I've heard. Any special women friends?" She tried to sound casual, but failed.

"None that I remember. Music's started. Shall we dance, Miss Fairchild?" He held out his arm and she accepted it. They strolled back toward the growing crowd.

"Hey, how long are we going to be courting, anyway?"

"Not long, why?"

He led her to the dance line. "I have my eye on another little filly."

The music started, and the gentlemen bowed. Isabel spotted Slade and Susannah, both watching her and Dusty. They spent the next hour responding to the square dancer's calls.

❧

"I figured out a way we can waltz, Susannah," Slade told her. "I've been working on an idea for square dancing, but I haven't come up with one yet."

Susannah grinned up at him. "I think both are equally impossible, but it's pure joy just to watch. Thank you for bringing us. Isabel is having the time of her life."

"Yes, it appears so. I think she's sweet on Dusty." He hated the fact that it bothered him and the fact he'd instigated it.

"And you're sweet on her?"

Slade sneered. "Me? Isabel? I think not."

"You never take your eyes off her." Susannah gave him that same knowing look his mother often used.

"You are imagining things. Isabel Fairchild is the last woman on earth I'd be interested in. She's impulsive—"

"And you, my dear brother, are too rigid. Perhaps you could balance one another the way God intended."

"She does love life," he admitted grudgingly. Watching her with Dusty pained him. He wanted to be the one swinging her around the dance floor, but why? A million things about her annoyed him, but they were the same qualities he admired. Her wit, her determination, her passion for Susannah.

"If she intrigues you, why do you treat her with such disdain? You constantly make your disapproval of her obvious."

"I do disapprove of her choices with you, but she disapproves of me just as much."

"Because of the choices you make on my behalf." Susannah chuckled. "Honestly, without me, the two of you would be perfect together."

"Neither of us would want to be without you. We both love you and want the best for you."

"You just don't agree on what that is."

"Exactly."

Finally the square dancing ended and the waltzing began. Slade grabbed Susannah's hand. "Come on. We'll show them how it's done."

Susannah pulled her hand out of his grasp. "No. I can't dance. I'll make a spectacle of myself and you."

"I've got it all figured out." He took her hand again and pulled her to her feet. "Trust me."

She rolled her eyes. "That's amusing coming from you. When is the last time you trusted someone?"

He only smiled at her and stopped on the edge of the floor. "Put your feet on top of mine."

"I thought the object when dancing was to keep one's feet off of one's partner." Susannah laughed but did as he asked.

"In most cases it is." Slade slowly waltzed to the music, carefully holding Susannah, keeping her steady. "But you are allowed."

Slade watched Isabel and Dusty across the room, laughing, talking, dancing. *Why is she under my skin? I don't even like her. Well, not much anyway.* But he did like her. Worse, he admired the tenacious way she fought for Susannah, even though he didn't agree with her ideas. And he admired the way she was willing to lose her job by fighting against something she believed an atrocity. As he observed her, he had a hard time remembering somewhere inside lurked a dance-hall girl. He couldn't picture her in that lifestyle.

At the start of the third dance, Dusty and Isabel drifted in their direction. "Mr. Stanfield, I'd like to cut in if you don't mind."

He stared at Dusty. What if he did mind? Could he trust him to be careful with Susannah? *Trust. There's that word again.* Slade carefully handed over his sister and took Isabel into his arms. He kept one eye on Susannah, worried about her being embarrassed.

"Shouldn't a gentleman pretend to be thrilled about his partner, even if it's untrue?"

Slade focused on those pools of emerald. "I'm sorry, Isabel. It's not you. This is Susannah's first social event since the accident. I'm concerned."

Her expression was compassionate, caring. "I understand. Dusty's concerned, too. I think she'll be fine."

Slade took one last gander; Susannah laughed, her face glowed, and she seemed completely comfortable with Dusty. "Guess I can trust Dusty to take care of her." He relaxed and floated through several songs with Isabel in his arms. With every breath, he inhaled the scent of lilac.

"Shall we take a break?" he asked, having lost all track of Dusty and Susannah.

"Yes, some punch would be nice," Isabel agreed. "They are over there in the shade." She'd caught him frantically searching. "You are worse than a mother bear." Isabel joined Dusty and Susannah while Slade obtained their drinks.

Slade returned with four small cups. "They are serving lunch—barbeque beef and Mexican beans—down at the tables under the grove of trees. Shall we?" he asked, offering his arm to Susannah.

"We shall. Dusty, why don't you and Isabel join us?"

Slade wasn't certain he wished to watch the happy couple, but he had no choice. He seated Susannah at a table, where Isabel joined her. He and Dusty went to get the food.

"Mr. Stanfield," Dusty began, then hesitated. "I've been giving Miss Fairchild the attention you asked me to, but what about Susannah, sir?"

"What about her?" Slade piled the barbeque beef onto his plate.

"I've heard several young men express interest in her. When will you allow callers?"

Slade nearly dropped his food. "Not for a while yet. We must see if she can keep up the pace of this normal life she's chosen." Slade felt certain all this business would take its toll, and Susannah would return to her subdued and protected lifestyle.

❧

"Isabel, what are your feelings for Dusty?" Susannah asked the moment the men were out of earshot.

Isabel shrugged. "He's very nice." Something in Susannah's eager expression made her ask, "What are your feelings for Dusty?"

Susannah blushed. "He used to call on me back before. . ."

Isabel squeezed Susannah's hand. "I'm not competition, if that's what you're asking. I'm gently letting your mother know I'm not interested in Slade by allowing her to think I am interested in Dusty. He's in on my scheme, and he's no more interested in me than I am in him."

Slade and Dusty returned. Dusty carried a plate for Isabel,

but nothing for himself.

"Why aren't you eating?" she questioned.

"The races will start soon. I must excuse myself and go warm up Lady."

Isabel could barely eat as the preparations for the first race began. In a small ring, Dusty led Lady, and the mare seemed to anticipate what lay ahead. She was dancing and snorting and tossing her head high.

"Do you think she'll win?" Isabel asked.

"She has as good a chance as any. Dusty's a good rider. Are you going to finish your lunch?" Slade asked.

"I can't. I'm too excited."

He gathered their three plates.

When he returned, he said, "Let's go sit on the grass over there." He assisted Susannah to a spot where they could all see well.

A bell rang, and all the riders for the first race gathered at the starting line. Spectators lined both sides of the track from beginning to end. Slade chose a spot near the end so they could all watch Lady cross the finish line first. Dusty struggled to make Lady stand still.

Someone shot a gun. The crowd shouted. The horses darted across the line and stretched their beautiful legs out and ran. Isabel's heart beat hard and fast. Lady sprinted out ahead. Isabel screamed and jumped. Slade was next to her, doing some yelling of his own. By the time Lady and Dusty crossed over the line, the horse was a full length ahead of the competition.

Slade grabbed Isabel, and they hugged while hopping up and down and shouting. "She won, Slade, she won!"

Slade pick up Susannah, and they ran down to congratulate Dusty. He and Slade patted each other's backs. Then Dusty hugged Susannah and Isabel.

"I have great news," he told Isabel when the excitement died down and they'd all hugged and patted Lady. "Mr. Ochoa offered to lend me his buggy for the race, and you, Miss Isabel, can be my partner."

"No, Isabel." Slade's voice came from behind her. "You can't do it. I will not allow you to!"

She whirled around and faced him. On the tip of her tongue was, *Slade Stanfield, I will not permit you to run my life the way you run Susannah's!* However, the terror in his eyes, the fear on Susannah's pale face stopped her.

Dusty hung his head. "I'm sorry, Mr. Stanfield, Susannah. I didn't mean to bring up any painful memories. If you'll excuse me, I'll inform Mr. Ochoa that we won't be needing a buggy after all."

"No, wait." Susannah stepped forward and grabbed Isabel's hand. Then she faced her brother. "Slade, we can't give in to our fear. It isn't right."

They all stood in a little cluster. Slade pale, staring at the ground. Dusty seemingly wishing he'd never mentioned the buggy race, and Susannah fighting the fear and digging deep for courage. Isabel studied each of their faces, and for the first time in her life was willing to forgo her desire for the good of someone else, for the good of people she cared about.

"Don't worry. Neither Dusty nor I mind backing out on Mr. Ochoa's offer."

Slade raised his gaze to meet hers. She saw surprise, gratitude, maybe even admiration. Her heart soared. That was enough for her. She smiled, both at him and at herself. Maybe she'd changed and had grown up some. Maybe her father would even be proud of her.

Slade cleared his throat. "Susannah's right. Please don't change your plans on our account."

seven

Isabel glanced from Slade's blanched face to Dusty's sorrowful eyes and back to Slade. "We don't need to race." She tried to lighten the moment. "We'll have a lot more fun spending the afternoon with you and Susannah." Isabel glanced over at Susannah; she leaned on Lady for support. "What do you say? Ready for more dancing?"

Susannah pasted a smile on her lips. "No. I apologize for my—our—reaction. You must race. Isabel, you are always in search of an adventure, and the buggy race is a great one. Momentarily, I panicked, but I'm fine. You must do it. Don't you agree, Slade?"

He cleared his throat and looked out over the horizon. "Know there are risks. Seems every year someone gets hurt. Susannah, however, has sustained the worst injuries so far."

A knot of anticipation developed in Isabel's midsection. She did ache to race. "What do you think?" she asked Dusty.

He stared at Susannah for a long time.

"Do it," Susannah whispered.

"All right." Dusty looked at Isabel. "You coming?"

She licked her dry lips. Her heart pounded. "I'm coming."

Susannah reached for Dusty, grabbing his arm. "Be careful."

He took her hand and squeezed. "I will," he promised. Dropping Susannah's hand, he offered his arm to Isabel.

"Hold on tight, Isabel," Susannah cautioned.

Isabel took Dusty's arm. "Guaranteed." She laughed. "My knuckles will be white from my death grip."

Slade said nothing as they walked away, but his expression told her he battled many emotions resulting from events three years ago.

Dusty led Isabel to the Ochoa barn. The large building smelled of hay and horses. Mr. Ochoa helped them harness a two-year-old sorrel filly to a two-wheel buggy. Isabel stroked the mare's velvet nose while the men adjusted straps and hooks.

"This gig is a new model and more lightweight than those built even ten years ago," Mr. Ochoa told Dusty. "The weight factor is an advantage. This cart won last year, though a different horse pulled it."

They led the small mare out of the barn. Her coat gleamed in the sunshine. Dusty patted her neck. "You're a pretty one, little girl."

"Her name's Henrietta." Mr. Ochoa straightened the reins and checked the harness one last time. "You're ready to go." He shook Dusty's hand. "Good luck." Then he tipped his hat in Isabel's direction. "Ma'am." He walked off toward the food.

"Henrietta? Who would name such a beautiful horse Henrietta?"

Dusty grinned at Isabel and shook his head.

"Mr. Ochoa," they said in unison.

Dusty lifted Isabel up into the gig and climbed in after her. "We are set up in one mighty fine rig, Miss Isabel. I think you and I will go home winners today." Dusty tapped the reins on Henrietta's haunches, and the mare pranced forward. He guided her to the spot where all the buggies gathered for the start of the first race.

Excitement coursed through Isabel, and she could hardly wait for the race to begin. She surveyed each of the other five teams that had entered various sizes and shapes of buggies. Theirs was the smallest and sleekest. Her hopes surged. "We're going to win. I just know," she whispered to Dusty.

He nodded and lined up at the starting line, holding the reins tight to keep Henrietta in her rightful spot. He spoke softly to the mare, trying to calm her.

Isabel spotted Slade, Susannah, and Mrs. Stanfield on a rise not far from the start and finish line. Feeling torn once again between her desire to experience the race and their pain, she smiled and waved. Only Susannah returned the gesture. Maybe this would help Slade realize the futility of worry.

"Are you holding on tight?" Dusty asked, keeping his eyes straight ahead.

"Yes." With not much to hold on to, Isabel tightened her grip. One hand wrapped around the gig frame and the other held tight to the edge of the seat between her and Dusty. Her hands were sweaty, and her grip was slippery at best.

Out of the corner of her eye, Isabel saw the starter raise the gun. She clutched harder to her anchors. The gun fired. Henrietta lurched forward. The gig followed. Isabel's head jerked back at the impact, then whipped forward. The wind stung her eyes, and she squinted, glimpsing rocks and trees as they flew by.

Her braids blew behind her, hitting against her back from time to time. Her hands ached from her tense grasp, but most incredible was her sense of almost flying. Isabel was moving faster than she ever had. "This is wonderful!" she yelled at Dusty, not certain he even heard. Between the wind in their ears and the hoof beats of six horses, the noise level was deafening.

Isabel looked around, trying to measure their lead. Henrietta led the pack but barely. The six racers were in a cluster, all sticking together and keeping the same pace. "We're winning!" Her competitive nature kicked into gear. "Can't she go any faster? They could catch us in a heartbeat."

Again, Dusty made no response. He kept his focus straight ahead.

Isabel caught sight of a black horse coming up on Dusty's side of the gig. With each breath, the horse moved closer to taking the lead. Isabel dug her fingers into the seat. They were so close, she knew Dusty could reach over and touch the horse if he chose to.

They hit a rut in the road. The gig bounced, and Isabel flew up off the seat. She lost her hold with one hand. Smacking back down on the seat, she clutched at the front edge once again. Her heart pounded and her mouth went dry. The black horse's nose was even with Henrietta's neck. Glancing back, Isabel felt fear wrap itself around her.

"They're too close!" she screamed.

In slow motion, Isabel watched the scene play out. The wheel of the passing buggy caught their wheel. Their buggy flew up in the air. Isabel shrieked. Unable to hold on, she shot through the air like a bullet. Sickened by the sound of crashing metal and squealing horses, she tried to focus her eyes on the noise. She hit the unrelenting ground in a heap. Her head jerked back. Something hard and sharp caught the back of her skull. The world spun, and a black void threatened to sweep her away.

Isabel tried to stay alert. She fought to open her eyes, but they wouldn't cooperate. Her head throbbed, and she felt warm liquid oozing down her neck. She tried to move, but her body refused to oblige. Her head hurt so badly. She gave up trying and welcomed the black fog that enveloped her.

❧

"No! Not Isabel," Slade yelled. He took off running. "Not Isabel. Please, God, not her, too." His boots pounded against the dirt. The sight of tangled buggies, flying bodies, and downed horses stuck in the forefront of his mind. The memories of three years before blended with the current happenings. By the time he reached the wreck, his whole body trembled with fear.

Mr. Ochoa and many others were digging through the debris of bent metal and broken harnesses to free hurt people beneath. As Slade neared the scene, he spotted Isabel. She'd been thrown away from the mess and lay off on the outside edge of the track. Her still form squeezed his heart with dread.

He didn't stop running until he'd reached her. Kneeling beside her, he checked her neck for a pulse. A sigh of gratefulness escaped his lips when he found the strong, steady beat.

"Isabel," he whispered. No response. He doubted he'd hear her anyway over the pounding of his heart and the loudness of his own heavy breaths.

He checked her arms and legs for breaks. Apparently, she was in one piece, but he noticed her head lay against a rock. Gently, he lifted it and felt for bumps. A huge knot protruded, and he felt blood dripping onto his hand. He removed the scarf from around her neck and tied it around her head to stop the bleeding.

"Lord, please heal Isabel. Don't let her have life-changing injuries from this like Susannah does."

Laying his palm against her ashen cheek, feelings of love overwhelmed him. He'd tried so hard, yet in spite of all his efforts not to, he'd fallen in love with Isabel Fairchild. "Lord, help me. I promised You I'd not fall in love for Susannah's sake. Now what do I do?"

He tenderly scooped Isabel into his arms; her auburn braids hung down and swung back and forth with each step he took.

"She all right?" Mr. Ochoa asked.

"Unconscious, but I think she'll be fine. Her head hit a rock."

"Why don't you lay her here and go get your buckboard? I'll have one of the women keep an eye on her."

Slade didn't want to leave her, didn't want her out of his sight, but he knew the suggestion was best. Gently, he placed Isabel on a soft mound of dirt. He carefully arranged her arms until she looked comfortable. "Don't go anywhere, Isabel. I'll be right back." He placed a kiss on her forehead.

"Any casualties?"

"Just my mare, Henrietta. Dusty is in pretty bad shape."

Dusty. In his panic over Isabel, he'd forgotten all about Dusty.

"Apparently he was trampled by a couple of horses and run over by a couple of buggies. His legs took the brunt of it. Both appear broken."

A sense of duty came over Slade. "Will you stay with her? Dusty's my foreman. I better have a look."

Mr. Ochoa nodded. As Slade moved toward the crowd of people, he heard the man yell, "Margarita, come sit with this woman."

Slade found Dusty. Doc Christiansen was with him. Susannah held one of Dusty's hands, and his mother held the other. Bloodied and bruised, Dusty was thankfully conscious.

"Isabel?" Dusty rasped out her name.

Slade knew talking pained him. "She's fine." *At least I hope she is.* He didn't want Dusty feeling worse than he already was.

Susannah had been crying, and his mother appeared scared stiff.

"What's the prognosis, Doc?"

"Both legs are broken. He's bruised. I'm trying to splint him good, and then we'll haul him up to the Ochoas' house. Ramon said he's welcome to stay here as long as he needs to. I think it will be a few days before he's making the trek back to your place. Miss Susannah volunteered to stay and care for him."

Slade frowned at his sister. She could barely take care of herself. How had she gotten down here anyway? Why did she run to Dusty and not Isabel? Slade didn't take time to ponder these questions further. "I'm going to get the buckboard and pick up Isabel. Doc, when you're done here, would you mind taking a look at the woman over there?" He pointed to Isabel's still form.

Doc nodded.

Slade jogged back toward the Ochoas' barn area, where he'd parked the buckboard. *Why did I let her and Dusty race? Why didn't I stop them?* He wrestled with God every step of the way, asking a million questions. God remained silent through the whole interrogation.

Slade rushed through hitching up the horses and returned to Isabel as quickly as possible. Doc knelt beside her. "She's bruised and sore and has a big goose egg on her noggin, but I think she'll be up and about in a few days."

As Slade drew closer, he realized Isabel's eyes were open. His heart swelled with relief. He ached to take her into his arms but couldn't. He'd promised himself and God. His love for Isabel must remain unacknowledged.

Doc helped her drink a few sips of water. "I think she's

ready to make the trip back to your place." Doc rose. "Travel slow, and try to avoid jolts as much as you can. Her headache is pretty intense."

Slade nodded and stooped next to her. Isabel touched Slade's cheek. "Doc told me about Dusty," she whispered. Tears gathered in her eyes. "Please forgive me for wanting to race. It's my fault he's hurt. I'm so very sorry."

He took her hand in a tight clasp. "It's no one's fault, Isabel." *Except maybe God's.* "You ready?"

"I don't think I can get up."

Slade laughed. "Always Miss Independent. I planned on carrying you."

Isabel smiled. "Please be careful. Every inch of my body hurts."

Slade lifted her, and she groaned. He stopped moving and stood still for a moment. Then he took small, careful steps. When he reached the wagon, he laid her across the back. Then he climbed in and situated her in the center of the straw.

"I'll be back as soon as I find my mother and Susannah."

Isabel touched his cheek again. "Thank you."

He kissed her hand. "You're welcome."

❧

Susannah knew Slade would fight her decision to stay with Dusty, so she mentally prepared herself for the battle. She'd suspected that she loved him even before her accident. She'd had many callers, but he was the one she wished for and thought about.

After her accident, she hadn't wished to see anyone, especially not him. How could he ever want a woman who wasn't whole? He'd tried to visit several times, but Slade had chased him off. Then, she'd been grateful, but once she worked through her grief and accepted this as God's plan for her life, she felt differently. She did want Dusty to call, yet he'd given up long ago. However, not one day passed that thoughts of Dusty didn't slip into her mind and heart.

The evening when she, Slade, and Isabel had run into Dusty down by the barn, all the emotions Susannah had carefully tucked out of sight hit her with the force of a train. She loved him still. Now, seeing him broken and battered tore at her until she wondered if her heart was literally bleeding. She must tell him how she felt. He had to know.

What if he has no such feelings for me? What if he really is attracted to Isabel?

No, I'll not give in to this fear. If he chooses Isabel, he chooses Isabel, but I'll not be a coward and avoid speaking the truth to him.

Slade approached. "Dusty, I have to get Isabel back to the ranch." Slade squatted next to the injured man. "Doc says you need to stay here for a few days. I'll be back for you when Doc sends word."

Dusty nodded.

"Ladies, are you ready?" He looked at Susannah in his pointed way.

Dusty's hand tightened around hers. The action warmed her heart.

"Susannah." Dusty ground out her name through tremendous pain. "Stay."

She looked at Slade. He looked at Mother. Mother rose and nodded. She kissed each of Susannah's cheeks. Mother smiled in her knowing way and walked with Slade back to the buckboard.

Doc and several of Mr. Ochoa's hired hands lifted Dusty onto a board and then into the back of a wagon. Doc then lifted Susannah up, where she settled next to Dusty, holding his hand for support. How she wished she'd allowed him close to her after her accident. How awful he must have felt when she shut him out.

❧

"Mama, is there something between Susannah and Dusty?" Slade asked on their walk to the buckboard.

"No, *mijo,* they are *amigos.* Only good friends. At least that is Susannah's belief. What about you and Isabel? You run to her like a man in love."

"I'm responsible for her while she's in my employ. Concern drove me, not love."

He lifted his mother into the back of the buckboard where she could keep an eye on Isabel. He held the horses to a slow pace, carefully avoiding the ruts and potholes along the way. Occasionally, Isabel groaned. The creaking of the wagon and the plodding of the horses weren't enough to keep his mind off his growing feelings for her.

Thoughts of her infiltrated his mind during the journey home. Her laughter echoed through his memory. Visions of her sopping wet, stepping up from the pond. Teaching her to ride. Holding her close. Dancing with her. Kissing her. And kissing her again. He attempted to rein in the wayward thoughts, but all he could think of was Isabel. Witty, charming Isabel. Fun-loving, adventurous Isabel. He'd almost lost her today, and the thought nearly killed him, but she wasn't his to have, wasn't his to love.

Arriving home, he stopped the buckboard in front of the house. His mother helped him as he carefully lifted Isabel from the straw-filled wagon and carried her into the house. Isabel winced with pain, and unshed tears filled her eyes. Her breathing was ragged.

"Lay her on the settee," his mother instructed. "I'll clean

her up and help her into her night clothes before I turn down her bed."

He did as directed. "I'll take care of the horses and then help you settle her into bed." Unable to help himself, he placed an angel-soft kiss on Isabel's forehead. Her startled, pain-filled gaze met his. Her eyes, filled with questions he couldn't answer, probed his face.

"I'll be back," he promised, wishing he could say more yet knowing there was nothing he could freely say—not today, not ever.

Isabel barely nodded and closed her eyes. How he wished he could take her pain and make it his own. Truth be known, it was already his own.

eight

"I know this hurts, Isabel, but I have to get you out of these dirty, bloody clothes and clean you up so I can get you into bed."

Isabel groaned as Mrs. Stanfield sat her up to remove the vest and clean the wound on the back of her head. "Never. . . hurt so. . .before."

"You're pretty banged up, but at least nothing is broken."

"Why, God. . ."

"Isabel, God didn't do this to you just like God didn't amputate Susannah's leg. We live in a fallen world. We take risks and bad results sometimes occur."

Isabel's father would have responded the same way if he'd been there. He often said, "God uses pain to get our attention, but He doesn't cause the pain." *But if He's God, couldn't He stop the pain?* How did Susannah manage joy and peace in the midst of her daily trial? Isabel felt neither of those emotions.

Mrs. Stanfield unbuttoned Isabel's blouse and helped her into a clean flannel gown. The nights were now pretty chilly. By the time she was done, tears streamed down Isabel's cheeks from the intense pain that every movement brought.

"Your whole body is bruised. I don't mean to hurt you. There's no other way." Mrs. Stanfield laid pillows on the settee, and Isabel leaned back against them. "I'll go start dinner. In the meantime, you just rest here. I'll have to have Slade lift you into bed a little later."

Isabel closed her eyes. Slade. He confused her. Her emotions around him confused her. Today he was so tender, so gentle. His eyes bore her pain, but then she'd heard what he'd said to his mother. *I'm responsible for her while she's in my employ. Concern drove me, not love.* Maybe the feelings she stirred in him were nothing more than concern, but the feelings he stirred in her ran much deeper.

"Isabel?"

She must have dozed off. Slade's voice speaking her name awakened her. His warm breath caressed her cheek. She'd been dreaming of him, and when she opened her eyes, Slade's face was mere inches from hers. Her heart beat faster. Moving her arm caused her to wince, but she had to touch his face and make sure he was real. She ran her fingers over his whiskered cheek. Slowly, very slowly, she traced his jaw line down to his strong chin.

His breath left his body in a whoosh. "Isabel." He turned his head and kissed her palm. "I'm so glad you're alive."

"Me, too." Her words came out in a moan.

He threaded his fingers through hers.

Isabel bit her bottom lip.

"I'm hurting you. I'm sorry." Slade laid her arm across her stomach and ran his hand over his hair. "All I could think about was how much I wanted you to see the ranch in the springtime. It's my favorite time of year and more beautiful than you can imagine."

Isabel focused on his warm eyes.

"Close your eyes and picture every shade of green imaginable. Can you see the fields covered in velvet soft grass?"

Isabel knew the beauty would take her breath away, but since talking hurt, she only listened.

"The hills are covered with wildflowers. Newborn colts

and calves fill the pastures." Slade's voice carried a smile. "I want you to be here, Isabel, and share all this with me."

Isabel opened her eyes and forced a smile, a tiny one, but a smile nonetheless.

"You want that, too. I can tell, so we have to get you well."

"Mmm," she groaned her agreement.

"Have you ever seen a cow give birth?"

She turned her head an inch or so to the left and then back.

"No? Well in some ways birth is a cruel thing. Usually the calves fall into the world headfirst. Being limber, they are almost always fine, but can you imagine having your first meeting with the earth be such a hard blow?"

She blinked twice.

"I understand. One blink for yes and two for no."

She blinked again—once.

"Then the momma cow faces her calf with this lovesick look in her eyes. She makes a strange rumbling, moaning sound—partly triumphant, partly anxious—as she waits for her baby to stand for the first time." Slade chuckled. "Picture a damp calf trying to stand on stick-thin legs, usually very wobbly legs that appear too long for the rest of its body. You have to be here for that, Isabel, and for the birth of the colts, too."

She blinked once. "Love. . .ranch?"

"Do I love this ranch?"

Another blink.

A faraway expression settled on his face. "I love everything about this ranch—the land, the livestock, the memories, the stories."

"Stories. . ."

"You want me to tell the stories?"

She blinked once. Blinking was about the only activity that didn't hurt.

"My great-grandfather Miguel Sanchez received a land grant from the Mexican government. He was given Rancho San Miguel, and his closest friend, Jose Ochoa, received the parcel next to ours."

Isabel blinked once. She remembered his mother telling her that this morning.

"My great-grandparents had many daughters—a dozen—before they finally had a son. The son, my grandfather, the sole heir to the *rancho,* married Jose Ochoa's youngest daughter. They loved each other deeply and worked the land together but had much difficulty producing a living heir. My mother was born in their old age—much like Isaac being born to Abraham and Sarah—but of course my grandparents weren't in their nineties. They were almost forty.

"They thought the sun rose and set in my mother's eyes. When she was sixteen, they carefully arranged a marriage for her with a man from back East. He had the maturity and education to take the ranch far. My father was a good man, a kind man. Sadly, he and my mother faced the same struggles her parents had regarding children.

"They were married nearly twenty years before I came along. My father put my mother to bed the minute they knew I was on the way, and he hired servants to wait on her until I arrived. He did the same thing with Susannah. My mother was thirty-five when she had me and thirty-nine when Susannah came. My father was already fifty and only lived until I was ten.

"He gave Susannah and me a love for books, music, and knowledge. My mother gave us a love for the land, the Lord, and family."

Mrs. Stanfield entered, carrying a bowl of soup. "Are you hungry, *mija?*"

Isabel blinked once.

"She says she's starved," Slade answered for her.

Mrs. Stanfield gave her son a puzzled frown.

"One blink is yes, two is no."

"Si." She handed Slade the soup and a spoon. "Do you mind? I need to finish the rest of our supper."

He'd never fed anyone before. With great care, he spooned the warm liquid into Isabel's slightly opened mouth. She ate slowly, closing her eyes and resting between bites. Somehow caring for her brought out even more feelings of tenderness. What was he going to do about Isabel Fairchild?

❧

Hard pressed to believe a week had passed, yet feeling every weary minute of the past seven days, Susannah laid her cheek against Dusty's forehead. Sure enough, his fever had finally broken. She let out a sigh of relief and rubbed the back of her neck. Today would mark a turning point in his recovery; the breaking of a fever always did.

Doc kept him pretty doped up on strong pain medication, hoping to keep him still as possible and give the bones a chance to mend. Both Dusty's legs were wrapped in splints, and Doc had wrapped his ribs as well. He had two black eyes and bruises over every part of his body that Susannah could see.

Doc came into the Ochoas' parlor. They'd turned it into a makeshift hospital room for Dusty. "How's my patient today?"

"Better. Fever's gone."

Doc's bushy brows drew together in a frown. He laid the back of his hand against Susannah's forehead. "You don't look so good yourself. You feeling all right?"

She let out another sigh. "Just weary."

"You've been a fine nurse, feeding and caring for my patient."

"It feels good to be useful again. Three years is a long time not to be."

Doc nodded. "I hope this proves to you and that bull-headed brother of yours that you are a whole person. Losing a leg doesn't mean you can't live a normal life. Why, you could even be a wife and mother if you chose."

"A wife?" She glanced at Dusty. "And a mother?" Hope bubbled up inside. "How?"

Doc chuckled. "I'm guessing you're asking how you could run a household."

"Yes. I fed Dusty, but the Ochoas' cook prepared the food."

"You'd be surprised what you could do if your mother and Slade would give you half a chance. I'm certain you could run a home as efficiently as any other woman. It may take you awhile longer, but you're more than capable."

Emotion welled up in her, and she threw her arms around Doc's sizeable middle. "Thank you," she whispered. "You have no idea the gift you've given me."

Doc chuckled and hugged her back. "You're welcome. Now, let's take a look at my patient." He checked Dusty over, and Dusty winced and groaned. "I'd like to see how he does without these." Doc pointed at the pain medication. "If he can handle the discomfort, I may send you two back to your ranch in a day or so."

Susannah nodded and grinned. It would be good to be home.

"I'll stop by in the morning."

"Bye, Doc."

When the door closed, Susannah took her chair next to Dusty. She laid her hand on his. "Did you hear?" she whispered. "Doc says I can be a wife and a mother! But do you think anybody would really want me?" Somehow she'd let her mother and Slade convince her she was doomed to the life of an invalid, but now she knew better.

Lord, You know my feelings for Dusty. Could he feel the same toward me? If marriage is in Your plans for me, I ask that You would fill his heart with love just for me.

❧

Slade had barely seen Isabel the past week. He worked from before sunup until long after sundown to keep up with both his and Dusty's jobs. He missed his foreman more than he'd thought possible. He missed Isabel, too, but knew staying away was best for both of them. He'd seen too many questions in her eyes, and she was frank enough to ask.

His good sense had returned, and he knew there was no room in his future for Isabel. He had to take care of Susannah and now probably Dusty, as well. The man had been loyal to them for four years and had no family. Slade felt responsible.

The sun had yet to rise over the eastern mountains, and he had more work than daylight hours. Opening the barn doors, he was greeted by the horses' neighs and snorts. Daisy mooed. Slade headed for the straw shed and collided with Isabel. He grabbed her upper arms to keep her from falling, and she cried out in a painful yelp.

"What are you doing out here?" he demanded, his tone gruff and annoyed. As soon as her stance steadied, he moved away from her.

Her pain-filled expression changed into one of hurt. "I thought I'd help you out until Dusty's back on his feet."

He scoffed. Seeing her, accidentally touching her, left him vulnerable, so he forced an arrogant, uncaring attitude. "What do you know about ranching? What do you know about work for that matter?"

Isabel raised her chin, and he noted the determination in her eyes. "I know your mother, your grandmother, and your great-grandmother all worked on this ranch. I may not know anything about ranching or work, but I'm willing to learn. Now, if you'll excuse me, I'll ask your mother to show me some chores I can do to help out."

All he needed was his mother involved. "Fine, Isabel. You want to work; I'll give you work." He'd give her so much work, she'd quit the first day. Bumping into her fifty times a day was the last thing he needed or wanted.

"I'm volunteering to help you out. You don't have to be rude. Your mother's worried about you working sixteen-hour days. I offered to assist you for her peace of mind."

"I thought you were still in bed, nursing aches and pains." He led her to the stall inside the big old building.

"I'm still sore in some spots, like the bruise on my upper arm, but a week does a lot for a battered body."

He wished he could tell her how thankful he was that she'd healed, but what good would it do either of them to be kind to one another? Caring would only make their inevitable good-bye harder. He'd make her glad she was leaving in less than four months, glad to see the last of him.

"The horses spend the daylight hours in the south pasture. About four in the afternoon, they have to be rounded up and led in here. They each have their own stall where they spend the night."

Isabel nodded, and he knew from her expressive face that she wondered how in the world she'd round up ten horses and get them safely into the barn. He'd leave her to solve the problem herself. He didn't want her back out there tomorrow.

"Morning starts before dawn on a ranch. First thing you do is feed the horses fresh hay. While they are eating, you milk the cows." He led her toward the straw shed, grabbing two pitchforks on the way out the barn door.

"Where do I get the hay?"

"I'm taking you there now." He showed her where the hay was stored. "You feed them the hay." He pointed to his left. Then pointing to the right, he added, "And use the straw to line the stalls after you clean them out." Slade handed her a pitchfork. He stabbed his into the hay pile and walked away carrying a breakfast-sized portion. He paused after a few steps, waiting for Isabel to do the same.

Sticking her pitchfork in the pile, she raised it, but most of the hay fell off. She tried again with the same result. Sighing, she gave it another shot, stabbing harder. This time she pulled up a fair amount of hay. Slade nodded his approval and led the way back to the hungry horses.

He carried his hay all the way to the last stall where Buck waited, then chucked the horse's breakfast over the fence. Isabel crept around the corner, trying hard to keep the hay balanced at the end of the pitchfork. Her face reflected ardent concentration.

"Go ahead and throw yours over the first stall to the big black gelding."

Isabel paused, looking at the five-foot fence and back at the hay perched precariously on the end of the long-handled tool. "You want me to throw the hay up and over the fence."

Slade nodded and moved toward her. "There's a feed trough—"

Isabel gripped the handle tighter, rotated, and swung. The hay flew up and plopped back down all over her.

"In the corner." Slade finished his sentence with peals of laughter.

Isabel had hay everywhere except in the feed trough. She joined him in his laughter, then picked hay off her clothes and out of her hair while Slade used the pitchfork to clean up the hay and feed the gelding. They returned to the shed for another round. Slade fed seven horses to Isabel's three. He chuckled. This job alone would take her hours.

Next, Slade led her to Daisy. He grabbed the pail, sat Isabel on the stool, and guided her through the milking process. He held her hands as they pulled the teats. Once the milk started flowing, he let Isabel do the work unassisted, although she struggled to milk as competently on her own. He had to put some distance between them. *Don't think about her smooth hands and velvety skin. Don't think about how good it would feel to wrap her in your arms. Just don't think!*

Once Isabel finished the milking, they visited the chicken coop for the day's egg supply. "After you have the milk and eggs, you carry both buckets up to the house to my mother." Slade carried the milk and let Isabel carry the eggs.

"Isn't it nice to have a helper, Slade?" his mother asked as he entered the kitchen.

He wanted to point out he was already running almost an hour behind but couldn't bring himself to be any ruder than he already had been.

"I think, so far, I've been more of a nuisance than a help," Isabel admitted.

Slade's mother took the pail of eggs and patted her arm. "At least you're trying. That's more than most women would do, isn't it, Slade?"

"It sure is." She had him there. Few women would even attempt what Isabel had tried to learn in one day. He grudgingly admired her tenacity. "We still have quite a few chores left. Let's go."

Isabel followed him back outside. "What's next?" she asked.

"We move the horses to the south pasture. They should

have finished their breakfast by now." Once in the barn, he showed Isabel where the halters and lead ropes were stored. He helped her do the first one, then she waited while he caught a second horse. They led them together to the pasture and turned them lose.

"Why do you feed them if they'll be out on the pasture all day?" Isabel asked on their way back to the barn for two more horses.

"I only give them about half their daily food supply. The other half they get out here. When the fields are green, I let them get all their food on their own, but rations are harder to come by this time of year."

Slade caught his second horse and waited while Isabel fought with the halter. She finally got it buckled, and they walked back out to the pasture.

"Thanksgiving is next week," she commented idly, but somehow Slade knew this conversation had a purpose.

"Mmm," was his sole response.

"I saw in the newspaper that on Thursday, November 29—Thanksgiving evening—there is a grand ball in Armory Hall."

He knew she planned on roping him into taking her. "No, Isabel."

"No, there isn't a ball?" she asked in innocence, batting her eyes.

"No, there might be a ball, but no one from this *ranchero* is attending."

"Slade, it's only $1.50 per couple, including supper. Your mother would get a much-deserved day off."

She was trying to ply him with guilt about how hard his mother worked. Make him think this was all for Mother's benefit.

"Is that the whole reason you're out here helping—because

you hoped to shame me into letting you have your way?" Slade was angry.

"No. One has nothing to do with the other."

Slade doubted her but said nothing more.

After helping Isabel clean out the first stall, Slade left her to clean the rest of the stalls and the water troughs. Next she'd put out fresh straw and carry in fresh water. Those jobs would consume most of the rest of the day. He was thankful she'd be out of his way. He would not take her to any dances or hold her again. He would not!

nine

Dusty had been alert for the past two days, but Susannah's courage abandoned her. She'd planned on sharing her feelings with him, but he seemed different now, more distant and pensive.

"Slade's coming to get us this morning."

Dusty nodded but said nothing.

"I'm more than ready to get back home. I'm certain you are, too."

"I have no home, Susannah." Pain resonated through his declaration.

"Of course you do. Rancho San Miguel is your home as well."

"No, Rancho San Miguel was where I worked. It was never my home." His words left knife-sharp imprints on her heart. "I'm going to write my aunt in Kansas and see if I can stay with her. I've saved a little money over the years, so I can buy myself a one-way ticket."

Susannah wrapped her arm around her midsection and limped to the window, leaning heavily on her cane. Tears blurred her vision. All the words she had planned on saying to Dusty would now never be spoken. All the love in her heart would never be returned. Dusty would leave and never know. He'd never know.

The parlor door burst open, and Slade walked in. "Good morning!"

Susannah swiped at her eyes before facing him. She only

nodded to acknowledge him, fairly certain words wouldn't squeeze past the lump in her throat.

Dusty said nothing at all.

Mr. Ochoa and several of his sons entered. They helped Slade move Dusty from the bed onto a board. Then they loaded him into the straw-filled wagon. Susannah followed behind them, and Slade lifted her onto the seat next to where he'd sit.

No one spoke all the way home.

❧

Slade wondered what had happened at the Ochoas'; both Susannah and Dusty brooded and were uncharacteristically quiet. A couple of Mr. Ochoa's sons met him at the ranch to help unload Dusty. Mother had readied the guest room next to Slade's room. Once they had him in the bed, Dusty asked Slade to stay. Slade thanked everyone, and Mama and the Ochoas left.

"Would you shut the door? I'd like our conversation kept private between us."

Slade nodded and obliged.

Dusty shared his plans to return to his aunt's in Kansas. He gave Slade her information and asked him to send a telegram.

"I'm happy to do whatever you need." Slade settled into the chair at the side of the bed. "But you know, I was thinking about your loyalty to me and the ranch. I appreciate you and all your hard work. You're welcome to stay. We planned on caring for you and nursing you back to health. Then I thought you might want to discuss buying a little piece of the land for yourself. Someday, you'll yearn for a wife and young ones all your own."

Dusty looked away but not before Slade saw the pain in his eyes. He couldn't help but wonder if Dusty was in love with Isabel.

Slade rose. "You think about my offer. If you still want me to send the telegraph, say the word. But know we will care for you for as long as it takes."

"Send it." Dusty still had his face turned away, and his voice carried deep emotional pain.

"I'll take care of it in the morning."

Dusty was running from something or someone. Slade just wasn't sure who or what.

Slade headed out the door to unhook the team of horses from the buckboard. The trip to the Ochoas' had cost him a precious day of fence mending. Tomorrow he'd have to ride into town for Dusty. Isabel had taken over many of the daily chores. He didn't know what he'd do without her, and he didn't want to feel that way. He didn't think she'd stick with it, but she had. He shook his head. She'd moved into his life, then his head, and now his heart.

❧

Isabel knew the minute Susannah hobbled into the house that she'd been crying. While the men took Dusty into his room, Isabel followed Susannah into hers.

"I missed you. Do you mind if I come in for a visit?" Isabel stood in the doorway.

"I'm afraid I won't be good company, but you're welcome to join me as long as you don't expect interesting conversation."

Isabel closed the door and situated herself on Susannah's settee. Susannah sat on the edge of her bed, appearing exhausted. "Why don't I come back later, after you've had a chance to rest?" Isabel rose.

"No, don't leave." Tears streamed down Susannah's cheeks. Isabel moved over next to her on the bed and wrapped her in a hug. She wasn't sure what to say or do, so she simply held Susannah and let her cry.

After many minutes, Susannah said, "Dusty's leaving." More tears fell as she told Isabel the Kansas story.

"Susannah, are you in love with Dusty?"

She nodded and wiped her tears on a lace handkerchief.

"Does he know? Have you told him?"

"I planned on at least dropping a few hints. The way he held me and looked at me and treated me when we waltzed led me to believe he felt something, too, but since the buggy wreck, he's barely said three words to me." Susannah limped the length of her room.

"I know he's probably dealing with grief, just like I did when I lost my leg, but he won't even talk to me. I've tried."

"I'll go talk to him, see what I can find out."

Panic filled Susannah's face. "Please don't tell him how I feel. I couldn't bear the embarrassment if he thought I was in here pining away for him."

"I'll show the utmost restraint." Isabel patted the bed. "You lie down for a nap. We'll talk again when you awaken."

Susannah lay across the bed, and Isabel covered her with a light quilt.

Isabel knocked on Dusty's door. When he answered, she opened it and stood in the doorway. "I just wanted to say hello. See how you are feeling."

"How do you think I'm feeling, Isabel? I can't walk, can't work. I'm worthless."

A knot of tears formed in Isabel's throat. She hadn't thought about how hard this might be on a man. "Dusty, please don't say such things. You're still the same wonderful man. This accident is a temporary setback."

Dusty shut his eyes. "Please shut the door. I prefer to be alone."

Isabel did as he asked. She went to her room and cried.

This was the first time in her life she recalled feeling other people's pain so intensely. She cried for Dusty and Susannah and over the hardships in their lives. "God, if You are there, if Your are who my parents believe Your are, please heal the hurts of my two friends. Please touch their lives and bring hope."

Glad she had chores to do to keep her mind occupied, Isabel washed her face and headed down toward the barn. "I wonder why life turns out the way it does," she commented to Lady as she led the mare back to a stall filled with fresh straw and clean water. She rubbed the horse between her eyes and kissed her velvet nose. "Someday, I hope to own a horse just like you."

She turned and ran into Slade. Heat rushed into Isabel's cheeks. He'd not only caught her talking to a horse, but kissing her!

Slade lifted an amused brow.

"Tomorrow I'm going to town to send Dusty's aunt a telegram and pick up the Thanksgiving supplies. Do you think you can handle everything around here?"

"I think I can. Would you mail another letter for me? I need to inform my family that I never made it to Arizona."

"Just a temporary setback," Slade reminded her.

"Maybe." She doubted she'd ever make Arizona. No longer even sure she wanted to, Isabel thought she might return home next spring and make things right with her family.

❧

Thanksgiving arrived the following week, but it seemed no one felt very thankful. The house was glum, and Slade had no idea how to reach Dusty, or Susannah, for that matter. Isabel spent more and more time outdoors. She'd take hours brushing the horses and caring for them. The woman never ceased to amaze him. He smiled just thinking of her.

When Mama called them in for dinner, he and Isabel walked back to the house together. She seemed content, and working in the sun had darkened her skin a few shades. He saw a few new freckles across her nose, and she had a healthy glow about her.

"I love this time of year—the briskness in the air," Isabel commented, raising her face to the sky.

"Me, too," he agreed.

When they got to the house, Mama and Susannah had Dusty at the table, though he didn't appear any too happy to be there. They'd put him in the wheelchair Susannah had used.

"Today," Mama announced, "we'll eat in the dining room." She wheeled Dusty in there, and they all followed.

As they gathered round the food-laden table, Isabel asked, "Can we each take a minute to share what we're thankful for? It's an old tradition back home."

Dusty's scowl said he wanted no part of any such nonsense, but Mama agreed. "I'm thankful for my Lord Jesus Christ and for a son and daughter who fill my life with blessings. I'm thankful for Isabel and Dusty, who share our hearts and lives." She looked to Slade. *"Mijo?"*

"I'm thankful for each of you and this *ranchero."* He turned to Susannah, who sat to his left.

"For life," was all she said.

She looked across at Isabel.

"I'm thankful for Slade, who didn't leave me stranded in Los Angeles." She glanced at him, a smile gracing her lips. As usual, whenever she looked at him, his heart banged against his ribs. "And I'm thankful for you, Mrs. Stanfield. You've been like a mother to me—both kind and loving.

I'm thankful for you, Susannah, and your friendship, and Dusty, I'm so grateful you are alive and sitting at this table with all of us."

Jealousy crept into Slade's heart. He'd suspected there was something between Isabel and Dusty, but Isabel's words brought it out in the open. No more denying their mutual attraction.

Everyone waited for Dusty's response. He finally looked up. "I think I'll pass." Bitterness laced each word.

They finished the meal in silence. Apparently, no one knew how to respond to Dusty.

❧

The following two weeks passed in near silence. Dusty brooded. Susannah grieved over lost love. Isabel and Slade both worked themselves to exhaustion. She'd taken on a few new chores as she got faster and more efficient. Ranch work wore her out but fulfilled her, too. She loved the animals, and every day presented some new adventure.

On this day, she rode Lady out to where Slade worked in the far north pasture. His mother had sent Isabel with a picnic lunch. She planned to talk Slade into allowing Susannah to attend the Christmas ball. Susannah needed to see there were other possibilities, other available men.

Isabel followed Mrs. Stanfield's directions and finally found Slade. He mended fences. Lady neighed at Blacky, causing Slade to notice her approach. He stood and waited.

"Your mother sent me with your lunch," she hollered, still a ways off.

"Good. I'm feeling hungry and dreaded the ride back to the ranch." He took the basket containing their food and the blanket for them to sit on.

Isabel slid off and tethered Lady near Blacky.

"Bless my mother's heart." Slade spread out the blanket and then the food.

"Fried chicken, potato salad, even some chocolate cake," Isabel informed him.

"And fresh lemonade. All my favorites."

Isabel joined Slade on the blanket. "The ride out here is beautiful. I love this ranch more all the time."

Slade smiled. "Me, too. There's not another place on earth I'd rather live or die." He bit into a fresh, warm tortilla.

"You're lucky."

Slade nodded. "Isabel, I can't thank you enough for all your help. I'll pay you Dusty's wage, and you'll earn your passage to Arizona even quicker."

Isabel's heart dropped at the reminder that her life on the ranch was temporary. "If you don't mind, I'd like to stay for my full six months."

"Suit yourself," Slade said, but he acted like he'd prefer she leave sooner.

"Why don't you have ranch hands like Mr. Ochoa?"

"We've had a couple of lean years, so I had to let everybody go except Dusty. I hire grub-line workers during the branding season and for the cattle drive, but since this year has been much more prosperous, I'll hire a few regulars in the spring. Also, the Ochoa ranch is much larger than ours."

"I thought he got a land grant the same as your great-grandfather." Isabel speared a bite of potato salad.

"He bought up more land as time passed."

"Oh." Isabel bit into a chicken leg. "Did Dusty ever hear back from his aunt?"

"Yes, but she's failing herself and can't take care of him."

"The poor man has no one."

"He'd have us if he wanted, but he doesn't seem to." Slade

wiped his greasy fingers on a cloth his mother had enclosed.

"He's having a difficult time accepting his injury. I've tried to talk to him, and so have your mother and Susannah. No one can get him to respond. I feel just awful. I wish he'd let someone help him."

Slade cocked his head, and his brows drew together. Isabel saw the questions in his eyes, but he didn't say anything.

She laid down her picked-clean chicken bone. "What? What are you thinking?"

Slade stretched his legs out and propped himself on one elbow. "I just expected you to be more torn up over Dusty."

"I do feel awful." Isabel shrugged.

"I thought you were in love with him." Slade shook his head.

"You have the right emotion, but the wrong girl. Susannah is the one pining for Dusty."

He sat up straight. "Susannah? My little sister, Susannah?" The thought of her being in love apparently stunned him.

Isabel laughed. "Yes, Susannah. She's a grown woman, Slade. Did you think she'd never fall in love?"

"No." He relaxed a little. "In her condition, how can she care for a home and a man?"

Isabel rose to her knees and brought out the chocolate cake. "Because she's lame?"

Slade nodded.

"Doc told her you and Mrs. Stanfield have limited her abilities."

At the hurt expression on Slade's face, Isabel regretted so carelessly blurting out the truth. "I'm sorry. I didn't mean that quite the way it sounded." Isabel took a deep breath and tried again. "Doc believes Susannah is more than capable of becoming a wife and even a mother."

"He told you this?" Slade accepted the cake from Isabel.

"No, but he told Susannah." Isabel tasted the moist chocolate treat and thought she'd gone to heaven. The cake melted in her mouth. "Your mother is by far the best cook I've ever known."

Slade smiled. "That she is. Now back to Susannah. What have my mother and I done to limit her?"

"You do everything for her and protect her so much, she'll never meet a man who might love her. Doc encouraged her to become independent, to take care of herself."

From Slade's thoughtful expression, Isabel knew he weighed her words.

"And speaking of meeting men. There is a Christmas ball. . . ."

"You never give up, do you?" He looked annoyed.

"Slade, it's for Susannah. Don't you want her to live as normal a life as possible?"

ten

Did Slade want Susannah to live as normal as possible? Truth be known, he ached for that, yet the thought also terrified him. If Susannah met someone and married, maybe there'd be a chance for him and Isabel. He gazed into the green eyes studying him, and his heart ached—ached to touch her, to hold her, to tell her he loved her. He did love her. The observation startled him. He loved Isabel Fairchild. He grinned at the revelation.

"What's so funny?" she asked.

"Life. Life is funny." Slade leaned back on one elbow and stared at the blue sky. "My goal was to protect her and keep her safe, but I've realized I can't do that. Only God can." He leaned up on one elbow. "You deserve the credit for that revelation." He reached for Isabel's hand and squeezed. "Thank you, Isabel, for not giving up until I saw the truth."

Isabel's mouth dropped open at Slade's confession.

"Now, tell me about this ball," Slade encouraged.

Her whole face lit up. She really was beautiful. "The Grand Christmas Ball is at the Horton House on Christmas evening. It's more expensive than the Thanksgiving ball, though. For $2.50, a couple can dance the night away and eat supper."

"If I bought two tickets—one for my mother and Susannah, the other for you and me—would you allow me to escort you?"

Her eyes glowed. "You want to escort me?" she asked, astounded.

"Yes." Slade rose to his feet and offered Isabel a hand. His heart hammered in his ears when she put her hand in his. They faced one another. In Isabel's eyes resided all the longing he felt. Placing a hand on each side of her face, he drew her lips to his.

The awe on her face made him smile. He felt exactly the same way. "I think I've now been kissed by a man," Isabel whispered.

He kissed her forehead. "Maybe you should go back home so I can get back to work. I find you a bit of a distraction."

Isabel grinned. "It's taken you long enough. You've been distracting me since I first arrived here. See you back at the house." She started cleaning up their lunch mess, and Slade retrieved Lady. He helped Isabel into the saddle and handed her the blanket and basket.

Slade returned to work with a grin on his face. Maybe things would work out for Isabel and him. Just maybe.

❧

Isabel rushed home, wanting to tell Susannah the news, hoping to give her friend something to look forward to. She tethered Lady outside the house and ran inside.

"A Christmas ball? I don't think so. Thank you anyway, Isabel. Besides, who would dance with me?"

"Susannah, the fact that Dusty's aunt is failing hasn't changed his mind about leaving us as soon as he can travel and make plans. You need to get on with your life, and I guarantee you a missing leg won't stop men from requesting a spin around the floor with you. You're a beautiful woman, Susannah."

A tear slithered down Susannah's cheek. "I love him. It's not that easy. I don't want to meet someone else. I want him to get over his brooding and figure out he loves me, too."

"I'm sorry." Isabel hugged Susannah. "I'm being selfish and thoughtless. Of course you aren't ready to go dancing. I'll tell Slade it's too soon. He can escort me to another dance sometime, maybe in the spring."

Susannah pulled back and met Isabel's gaze. "Slade invited you to the ball?"

"I suggested the ball to divert your attention. Once he agreed, he asked me." Isabel knew her smile went from ear to ear.

"Oh, Isabel, I dreamed of this happening." Susannah hugged her. "Of course, we'll go. I don't want Slade to miss his evening with you." Susannah smiled for the first time in weeks. "Let's search my closet for two party dresses."

"Are you certain?" Isabel asked, concerned with Susannah's well-being.

"Indeed I am. Oh, Isabel, if Slade asked for your hand, would you give it?" Susannah clutched Isabel's arm, and they proceeded to Susannah's closet.

Isabel hesitated. Dare she put her feelings to words? "I think I would. I love the ranch, you, your mother, the animals. I find ranch life is a daily adventure."

Susannah's face reflected disappointment. "What about Slade, Isabel? Do you love him?"

"I love kissing him." She giggled.

"I know many people grow to love one another later, but, Isabel, I must know if you care for Slade even a little." Susannah sat on her bed, no longer interested in dresses.

Isabel grew serious. "I care for him very much. So much it scares me."

Susannah sighed. "I'm glad. I'd be saddened if that weren't the case." Susannah went back over to the closet and dug through the garments, pulling out several dresses. Sadly, they were all too short for Isabel, who towered over Susannah by many inches.

"Perhaps I'll wear my traveling clothes." She tried not to sound disappointed.

"You said you sew. Why don't you make something?"

"Perhaps I will. Now if you'll excuse me, I have an errand to take care of this afternoon. I'll be back by supper." Isabel headed outside, climbed back up on Lady, and rode to the Ochoa ranch.

"Good day," one of Mr. Ochoa's sons greeted her.

"Hello. May I speak to your father?"

He nodded. "Come into the house, and I'll get him for you."

Isabel took a seat on a horsehair sofa in the parlor and waited. She hoped her plan would work.

"Miss Fairchild, what a pleasant surprise. What can I do for you?"

"I'm here on an errand of mercy. Miss Stanfield has agreed to attend the Grand Christmas Ball, and I hope to ensure her dance card is full."

He frowned. "I'm a married man."

Isabel giggled and rose. "I wasn't thinking of you as much as your sons and your ranch hands."

Mr. Ochoa blushed.

"I hoped you'd *encourage* them to make sure she danced every dance."

He grinned. "I will do so. How thoughtful of you to watch out for your friend."

"Thank you, sir. I will most appreciate your help in this delicate matter. And you may wish to mention that in order for her to dance, she must stand on the gentleman's feet."

"I will take care of it. Might I offer you some refreshment before you leave?"

"Thank you, yes."

After a cool drink of water, Isabel rode back over the ridge to Rancho San Miguel. When she returned, she found Slade doing her evening chores.

"Where have you been?" He was furious.

"I rode over to the Ochoas'."

"Isabel, do you remember me requesting that you not leave the house without letting someone know where you are?"

Isabel nodded. "I'm sorry. Susannah knew—"

"Susannah knew you had an errand to take care of. Not which direction you went. What if something had happened? What if your horse threw you? No one would know where to begin to look, and what business could you possibly have at the Ochoa ranch?" Was Slade jealous?

"I rode over to request dance partners for your sister—to make sure she'd be busy all evening. Help take her mind off Dusty."

"Isabel, you can't just traipse off to the next ranch and order the hands to dance with my sister. Do you know how humiliated she'd be?"

"I didn't think—"

"That's the problem. You never think."

"No, I never do, especially when I let you kiss me." Isabel unsaddled and rubbed down Lady, boiling all the while. Then she helped Slade finish her chores but never said a word to him. How dare he act so bossy!

On the way back to the house after they'd finished, Slade stopped. "I'm sorry, Isabel. I was worried, and I don't like the idea of you making deals with a bunch of cowpokes."

"You're forgiven, and I didn't make any deals with *cowpokes.* I only asked Mr. Ochoa if he could make certain Susannah's dance card was full. It seemed the right thing at the moment."

❧

The following week at breakfast, Slade announced, "We're all going to town today." Then he looked pointedly at Isabel. "I've done the morning chores already."

"Why are we going to town?" Mother asked.

"Because we all need a break from the routine and because Marston's is having a winter clearance, and I know two young ladies who have no gowns to wear to the ball."

Slade enjoyed the delight on Isabel and Susannah's faces. They looked at each other and squealed. Dusty, on the other hand, mumbled something under his breath.

"Don't worry, we won't leave you behind. I've built a ramp so we can roll your wheelchair right up into the buckboard. Wouldn't dream of leaving you out of the fun."

Dusty wanted no part of their outing; the expression on his face made his stance clear. However, both Slade and his mother had learned a thing or two in the past three years, or at least the past three months with Isabel around. They knew Dusty needed to keep living, even though he didn't want to, so they insisted he go along.

The five of them loaded into the buckboard for a day in town. Isabel tried to get some singing going, but no one cooperated. Finally, she gave up and they made the trip in silence.

"Marston's is our first stop. While you ladies shop, Dusty and I will pick up some supplies. Then we'll pick you up and go to the Bandini House in the Cosmopolitan Hotel for some dinner."

All three of the women's faces lit up, and Slade chuckled, pleased to have pleased them. After dropping them off, he and Dusty headed for the general store. Mama had given him a list to fill. While the grocer handled the list, Slade rolled Dusty over to the café for a cup of coffee.

"How are you doing?" Slade asked after he'd taken a sip of the hot liquid.

"Fine." Dusty sipped his coffee. "I'm just fine."

"When you asked me about letting men court Susannah, who were you referring to?"

Dusty blanched. "Doesn't matter now. That man's gone."

Slade nodded and studied Dusty's bitter countenance. "You were the man, weren't you?"

Dusty glared into Slade's eyes. "Why are you doing this? Is your goal to kick a man when he's down?"

Slade ignored the comment and the anger. "If you'd have asked, I'd have said yes. If you asked now, I would still grant my permission."

Dusty attempted a laugh, but an embittered sound was all that came out. "Yeah, I was the one interested, but I didn't ask because I had nothing to offer the boss's sister. I have even less now."

Slade hurt for the guy. A man couldn't go to a woman empty-handed.

"I offered to sell you a piece of land."

"What if I never walk again? Doc says at best I'll limp. What if I can never work?" Dusty stared at his coffee, refusing to let Slade see the pain in his eyes. But the pain in Dusty's voice, Slade could never miss.

Slade decided to blurt out the truth. Maybe, just maybe, it would knock some sense into his friend. "Susannah fancies herself in love with you."

Dusty's head jerked up, and Slade saw the tiniest glimmer of hope on his face. "Did she say so?"

"She said so to Isabel."

Dusty took a long, slow swig of his coffee. "I've loved her since before she got hurt." His voice reverberated with pain.

"But she was always the boss's sister, and I was always just a ranch hand."

What do I say, God? How do I reach him? "I've never been class conscious. You're a hardworking man. That's enough for me."

"What if I can never work again? I can't even take care of myself, much less a wife."

"I understand." And the sad part was, he did. A man had a code of honor to live by. Part of that honor was providing for family. "I just wanted you to know the truth."

"I appreciate that and all you've done for me. At least now I have a reason to work hard to get out of this chair." Dusty almost smiled. "And now I understand why Susannah treats me like I have the plague. She doesn't think I care, but I do." He drained his coffee cup. "She's the reason I never moved on to another ranch. I kept hoping someday I'd find a way to offer her more than just my heart.

"Then when she got hurt. . ." His cracked with emotion. "I couldn't leave."

Slade remembered how almost daily Dusty had inquired about Susannah. Several times, he'd paid a visit, but Susannah never wanted visitors. Now the puzzle pieces fit together into a clear picture.

"When you're ready, I have a piece of land to sell you and a sister who loves you." Slade never expected this day to come, and he was overwhelmed with gratitude to the Lord.

Dusty nodded, and Slade knew he, too, was deeply moved by God's goodness.

Slade rose and wheeled Dusty back to the general store. After loading their supplies and pushing Dusty up the ramp into the buckboard, Slade returned to Marston's for the women. They waited outside, chattering like magpies.

A smile settled on Slade's lips. Today, all seemed right with the world.

❧

Isabel and Susannah had their dresses wrapped in paper so Slade couldn't see them until the night of the ball. They wanted to surprise him. This was the first time in the past month Susannah had shown any enthusiasm for life, and Isabel knew going to the ball had been a good choice.

While they waited in front of the store for Slade, they talked about the fashions they'd seen. Even Mrs. Stanfield had bought a new dress for the ball. "Times like these, I miss your father so much," she commented to Susannah.

"I miss him, too, Mama. Someday, I pray God will give me a man who'll love me as much as Papa loved you."

"And someday He will, *mija.*"

Isabel hoped that someday would be soon and the man would be Dusty. She couldn't help hoping a little for herself and Slade, too. Every time they made progress, something came along and knocked them backwards. Just thinking about him caused her heart to pitter-patter.

Slade pulled up on the buckboard. His eyes met hers, her heart jolted, and she smiled wide. *I love you, Slade Stanfield. I hope you figure out soon that you love me back.*

Slade climbed down and helped the women into the wagon. First, he laid their dresses on top of the supplies, then he assisted his mother onto the bench up front with him and helped Susannah and Isabel to get in the back with Dusty. His and Isabel's gazes were like magnets, constantly drawn to each other.

Once she settled in the back, Isabel noticed Dusty watching Susannah. Something had changed. A tiny chunk of his self-made armor seemed to be missing. His face appeared more vulnerable and less bitter. Isabel smiled to herself. Maybe he and Slade had had a talk.

The Bandini House was on the bottom floor of the Cosmopolitan Hotel. The hotel was one of only a few two-story buildings in San Diego. It was a wooden building with a balcony all the way around the second floor. "This looks more like it belongs in San Francisco than here," Isabel commented.

Slade agreed. "It's not even adobe."

Though the restaurant was crowded, the group was able to find a table for five. Isabel knew Dusty hated the stares and always kept his gaze on the floor. *Dear Lord, please give him his life back.* Isabel found herself praying more and more. *Does that mean I believe?* Yes, she knew she believed in God, always had. It was the personal relationship she really didn't understand. Her mother said God longed to be Isabel's best friend. How did one become best friends with God? Isabel would ask Susannah sometime when they were alone.

Mrs. Stanfield took the end seat, and Dusty and Slade faced Susannah and Isabel. After they ordered, they talked about the ranch and the ball. Even Dusty said a couple of things. Susannah smiled at Isabel, a hopeful expression on her face.

They all arrived home after a full day, tired but happy.

❧

"Susannah, would you take a walk with me?"

Susannah's heart stopped beating, then sped up double time. She turned to face Dusty as Slade rolled him down from the buckboard, wondering if she'd heard him right.

He watched her with expectancy.

She swallowed. "Did you ask me to. . . ?"

Dusty nodded. "Walk with me."

Slade rolled the wheelchair over to her, and she grasped the handles.

"Where are we walking?" she asked.

"Not far."

"That's a relief," she joked. "It's close to sundown." They must have made quite a pair, him in his chair and her limping along behind him. "The good thing about you being in this chair is I don't have to use my cane."

"That's the only good thing. Let's stop under the big oak there." They'd only gone a few hundred feet from the house.

After parking Dusty to face her, Susannah sat on the bench Mama had had Slade build. This was where Mama came every morning to meet with the Lord.

"Susannah, I'd like to escort you to the Christmas ball." Dusty grinned, looking a little shy. "Of course, you realize I won't be able to actually dance with you."

She reached for his hand. "Dancing doesn't matter to me. I'd rather be with you."

"Then I'll take that as a yes."

"A definite yes."

Dusty raised his head toward the sky. "Susannah, how did you learn to accept your accident? How can you always be so cheerful and happy?"

"I read the book of Job over and over. Each time, God did a little more work on my heart until I could say with Job, 'Though He slay me—yet will I praise Him.' "

"It's hard to feel like praising when my whole life is gone."

Susannah felt a lump tightening her throat. "I know." She lowered her head so he wouldn't see tears building in her eyes. "Believe me, I know. But I learned the more I praise Him, the more I want to." Susannah raised her gaze and saw the tears in Dusty's eyes as well. Hers spilled over and trailed down her cheeks.

"I wish I wanted to, but I feel so mad at God. Why? Why did this happen?" Dusty balled up his fist and pounded it into the open palm of his other hand.

"I don't know, but I do know that I appreciate God more than I ever have. I know Him better because, in my pain, I sought Him out."

"Were you ever mad?"

"Oh, yes. At first I was so mad I never wanted to see another human being or talk to God ever again."

"I came to see you many times, but you always turned me away." His quiet words brought her gaze to his face, his handsome, strong face.

"I wish I hadn't," she responded honestly. "Why did you keep coming? No one else bothered."

"Don't you know?"

She shook her head.

"I was once in love with you."

"Oh." His words settled into her heart like an anchor settles into the ocean—heavy and hard. *Was once* not *am still.* Once she lost her leg, he probably lost his interest.

Slade and Isabel approached from the barn, where they had finished evening chores. After a greeting, Slade pushed Dusty back to the house, and Susannah leaned on Isabel for support. She was glad they'd prevented her from responding to Dusty. She had no idea what to say.

eleven

Slade waited with his mother and Dusty on the front veranda for Isabel and Susannah. All three dressed in finery. They had celebrated Christmas by sharing their favorite Christmas stories and eating a huge breakfast. No gifts were exchanged, but tonight was Slade's gift to each of them.

When the front door finally opened and Dusty and Slade caught their first glimpses of Susannah and Isabel, there was a collective gasp. Both women were so beautiful—Isabel in her Christmas green silk gown and Susannah in her red velvet one. Isabel's hair was swept up in a bun on the crown of her head, while ringlets cascaded down her back. Susannah's hair was styled in a similar manner.

"Ladies," Slade announced, offering them each an arm, "your carriage awaits." He surprised them by borrowing one of the Ochoas' nicest coaches.

Isabel smiled up at him, making the surprise all the more worthwhile. "Oh, Slade, it's beautiful."

"And so elegant," Susannah added.

Slade helped each of them into the coach and then returned for his mother in her midnight blue gown. After she settled in across from the girls, Slade lifted Dusty into the closed carriage. Then he climbed in and shut the door.

"I've arranged for two drivers. One for us and one for the buckboard carrying your chair. Doc says a couple more weeks and you can start using those legs."

"I hope they still remember how to work." Though Dusty's

comment sounded offhanded, Slade knew the man wrestled with fear—fear he'd never walk or work again. Fear he'd never have anything to offer Susannah.

"They'll work. I've just got a feeling," Isabel stated.

Isabel never let life get her down. Slade loved that about her. Come to think of it, he'd been finding lots to love about her and less and less to dislike. He'd convinced himself Isabel wasn't really a dance-hall girl at heart. She was searching for herself, and he believed she'd found her place here at the ranch.

The girls spent the ride to town chatting about their favorite dances. Slade had worried no one would dance with Susannah, even though Isabel had tried to ensure that didn't happen. However, since Dusty asked to escort her, that didn't seem to matter so much. Slade guessed that if Susannah didn't dance once, she'd be happy as a lark in Dusty's company.

Once they arrived at the Horton House, they were directed to the dining hall, where dinner would be served before the ball began. Slade pushed Dusty into the room, while his mother and Isabel gave Susannah the support she needed.

"All the tables seat eight, sir," a servant informed Slade. "So other guests will be joining your party."

Slade nodded and pulled out a chair for Susannah and one for his mother. Lastly, he seated Isabel next to him and rolled Dusty up between Isabel and Susannah. The man who seated them removed the extra chair Dusty wouldn't need.

As the room filled up, three single gentlemen were seated at the Stanfield table. They showered attention on Susannah and Isabel. Slade glanced at Dusty and knew he felt possessive, too. Isabel made a point of drawing Slade into the conversation. She laid her hand on his arm, letting everyone know they were together. He appreciated the tactful way she handled the situation.

"Susannah, you and Dusty must forget trying to be alone tonight," Isabel said out of the blue. Both Susannah and Dusty appeared dumbfounded.

Slade chuckled, knowing she had insured the other three men knew the ladies at this table were spoken for.

"Aren't they the most handsome couple?" Isabel asked the man on his mother's right.

The man nodded his agreement. Dusty and Susannah both turned five shades of red. Mrs. Stanfield nodded at Isabel, apparently appreciating her shrewdness. Slade patted Isabel's hand, which still lay on his arm.

"Thank you," he whispered in her ear. "Susannah's rather protected life hasn't prepared her to handle all situations."

Isabel endowed him with her smile. "Protected life? Not Susannah."

"Point taken," he agreed.

After dinner, guests at each table were guided to the grand ballroom. Mrs. Stanfield went first, with Susannah leaning heavily on her for support. Isabel followed, and Slade trailed behind, pushing Dusty. The three men brought up the rear. The moment the three fellows noticed Susannah's limp, they commented a little too loudly, "No wonder she's with a lame fellow."

Another one laughed and said, "Why would two cripples pay money to go to a dance?"

Slade noticed Dusty tense. He tried to walk faster so they'd not have to hear anymore comments, but following Susannah made moving fast impossible.

"What if she'd been available and one of us got stuck with her all night?"

"Seems a little underhanded to sit at a table and look normal."

Slade spun around. "I suggest you all be quiet, or we will have to take this discussion outside."

"Your wheelchair friend coming, too?" one of them asked.

Mr. Ochoa stepped up. "Slade, is everything all right?"

"These men are mocking Susannah."

"Susannah? My cousin's daughter, Susannah? I think not." Mr. Ochoa signaled some of his men, and they helped the loudmouths out the door.

Slade knew the encounter had affected Dusty badly. How helpless he must have felt, unable to defend the woman he cared about. Slade wished he could change the facts, but truth was, he couldn't. All he could do was let the incident go.

❧

Isabel hoped Susannah hadn't heard the rude comments, but the expression on her pretty face denied Isabel's wish. "Don't worry. You're with the man you'd choose above all others, so who cares what they think?"

"I know you're right." Susannah raised her chin. "They can't ruin tonight for me."

"Good for you!"

Almost the minute they arrived in the ballroom, men swarmed around Susannah, asking her to dance. She appeared overwhelmed by the attention and looked to Dusty for the answer to her plight. He shrugged his shoulders, helpless to whisk her away from it all. Isabel realized this line of men was her doing. Now she wished she hadn't been so overzealous.

"Go ahead," Dusty said. "I obviously can't dance with you. One of us might as well enjoy themselves." The bitterness was back in his voice.

One of Mr. Ochoa's sons helped Susannah plant her feet on his and whirled off with her.

"Dusty, I'm sorry. This is my fault," Isabel confessed, feeling horrible. This was his second big blow tonight. "Once I convinced Susannah to attend the ball, I rode to the Ochoa ranch to line up a full dance card for her. I had no idea you'd offer to escort her. Had I, I'd never have meddled."

"This is a good reminder, Isabel. I have no business courting a woman. I can't even take care of myself, let alone protect Susannah." Dusty shook his head, sinking back into sullenness.

Isabel, Slade, and Mrs. Stanfield sat with Dusty for several songs while Susannah was passed from partner to partner. Isabel sighed her frustration. Watching Susannah laugh and enjoy herself did nothing to improve Dusty's mood.

"You don't have to sit here with me," Dusty said. "Frankly, I'd rather be alone, so if you don't mind, why don't you go dance or something?"

Slade stood and held out his hand to Isabel. She accepted. The orchestra played a slow waltz, so she slipped into his arms, and they glided across the floor. Mrs. Stanfield went to find some of her quilting friends.

"You know what I realized tonight?" Slade asked once they'd put some distance between themselves and Dusty.

"What's that?"

"Trying to control other people's lives always ends in disaster."

Isabel beamed at him. "Like the awkward situation I created tonight?"

"And like the problems I made during the past three years. I was foolish to think I could protect Susannah from all the hurts of life."

Isabel glanced back at Dusty. "I wish we could erase the hurt tonight has heaped on him."

"Me, too." Slade let out a long, slow breath. "At least she's having a good time."

Susannah's face glowed from pleasure and exertion.

"Mr. Ochoa certainly lived up to my request."

"Thank you for doing this for her." Slade spun Isabel around.

"Even though the plan blew up in Dusty's face?"

"I know you meant well, and I'm grateful." Slade stopped. "Do you want to get some air out on the balcony?"

"Some air would be nice." She sensed he wanted to tell her something important.

They spent a few moments in silence, enjoying the stars and the crisp night air. Finally, Slade turned her to face him. "Isabel, I've been wrong about many things—most things when it comes down to it. Would you forgive me?"

"For what? For loving your sister and doing what you thought best? There's nothing to forgive, at least not from me. Maybe Susannah might feel differently. I don't know."

"I was more thinking about the way I treated you and reacted to your suggestions."

"I forgave you long ago. I knew you only wanted your idea of the best for Susannah."

Slade's eyes darkened a shade. "I realize now you were a godsend. We all needed you, Isabel, but me even more than Susannah." He ran his fingers through her ringlets. "I'm so grateful for everything you've done for her benefit, even the line of men waiting to dance with her tonight." He kissed her cheek. "Thank you, Isabel."

Feeling choked up, Isabel replied, "You're welcome," but her voice sounded squeaky.

"Look at her, dancing and enjoying this wonderful, enchanted evening. You did this for her."

Isabel smiled, and a tear trickled down her cheek. She'd never received such high praise before, and, frankly, the words sounded wonderful. The deep appreciation Slade felt for her made her heart swell with love for him. All of her life, she'd longed for something, and tonight she realized it was gratitude and appreciation.

Her family loved her, but she'd always been the youngest one, the one in the way. Her mother and father had one another, and Gabrielle and Magdalene, who were close in age, had been close friends for years. Isabel had been so much younger and had no one who needed or appreciated her until now.

"Isabel, are you still planning that trip to Arizona?" The urgency in Slade's voice drew her attention back to him.

She shook her head, recognizing that her earlier plans simply grew from her search for men's admiration. Now she only wanted one man's admiration. And the way he looked at her, she believed she had it.

Slade bent his head to kiss her, tenderly holding her face in his hands. "I love you, Isabel."

Her heart nearly jumped out of her chest, and her knees felt weak. "You do?" She knew he thought highly of her and that she loved him, but she had no idea that he loved her.

"I do, and now that you've been kissed by a man, I plan to be the only man who ever kisses you again. Will you marry me?"

Stunned, Isabel's mouth dropped open. "Oh, Slade, yes! A million times, yes!"

She hugged him and rained quick kisses across his cheek.

He laughed. "That was another thing I failed to control—the love growing in my heart for you since about day one." He kissed her nose.

"I'm glad you gave up on the whole idea of trying to control life."

"Me, too. Now let's go keep Dusty company."

"Slade, can we wait to share our happiness until Dusty and Susannah figure out theirs?"

"That was my plan," he said as they reentered the hall.

❧

As they approached Dusty, Slade watched Susannah go up to him. The scowl on Dusty's face caused Slade's steps to slow. Dusty turned his chair and rolled away from Susannah and out another doorway.

"Maybe I should talk to him."

"I'll go console Susannah." Isabel pulled back on his arm. "Don't forget that I love you." She grinned, and her dimples danced across her cheeks.

"I won't." And he wouldn't. Slade was grateful to the Lord for Isabel. *The Lord.* He'd forgotten all about Him when it came to Isabel. What had he just gone and done? He'd asked Isabel to marry him without seeking God's leading. His stomach tightened up into a giant knot of worry. He hadn't prayed about marrying her; he hadn't prayed about much lately. Not much at all. "God," he whispered, "I'm sorry. We'll have to work this out later. Right now, I have another problem to address. Give me Your wisdom to share with Dusty."

Slade found Dusty all alone on a small porch. He knew the man had been crying by the redness of his eyes. His heart ached for Dusty, yet he didn't know what to say or do. "I thought I might find you out here." Not wishing to embarrass his friend, Slade made a point to avoid looking at him. Instead, he stared up at the moon.

"I made a huge mistake, Slade. I can't court Susannah or even think about marriage." Dusty's voice was flatter than one of Mama's tortillas.

"But you love her," Slade argued.

"That's not enough. I would become an anchor around her neck. She'd grow to hate me."

"Somehow I doubt that." Slade spoke quietly.

"Look at me, Slade! Look at me."

He did as Dusty asked.

"I'm half a man with no way to protect myself, let alone Susannah. Sometimes love isn't enough."

"I think love would be enough for Susannah." Slade knew he was fighting an already lost battle.

"Well, it's not enough for me. I'll be leaving the ranch as soon as I can manage a little better on my own."

Slade closed his eyes. Was God giving him a way out with Isabel? If Susannah wasn't getting married, neither could he. He'd made a promise. "Where will you go?"

"Doesn't matter. I just have to go. Please don't say anything about this to Susannah."

Slade nodded his agreement. What a mess their lives were in. Soon, there would be four brokenhearted people with hopes dashed and dreams lying dead at their feet. Once again, he and Susannah would be alone.

❧

"Isabel, am I wrong to dance and enjoy myself?" Susannah asked.

"Not since Dusty told you to go ahead. Problem is, he's hurting. How do you think he feels not being able to dance with you himself?" Isabel led Susannah out onto the balcony where Slade had just proposed.

"I know how he feels! But if he had the chance to dance for the second time in years, I'd encourage him." Susannah's face scrunched in frustration. "I'd plead with him to go and enjoy."

Isabel shivered and wrapped her arms around her middle.

"Would you have right after the accident, while you were still in your—what did you call it—grieving period?"

Susannah's face registered how true Isabel's words rang. "Maybe not," she admitted.

"Probably not?" Isabel asked.

"You're right, Isabel. I've been thoughtless. How much he must hurt watching me with other men. Please take me to him this minute. I must apologize at once."

Isabel guided Susannah to the door she'd seen Slade exit. They found the two men alone and in the midst of a serious conversation.

"Can we interrupt? Susannah has something she wishes to say to Dusty."

Both men waited expectantly, but Isabel spotted the worry in Slade's eyes.

"Maybe Slade and I should wait inside."

"No, it's all right if you hear." Susannah still clung to Isabel's arm. "Dusty, please forgive my thoughtless behavior tonight. I never considered your feelings. And I'm now undergoing deep regret for dancing the night away and ignoring you. This newfound freedom went to my head. Will you forgive me?"

"The truth is your choices tonight only served to make my decision easier. I had no business inviting you here tonight. I have no business courting at all." Dusty rolled his chair back into the ballroom.

Susannah's face puckered, and Isabel ached for the both of them. After all, she knew the joy of loving and being loved. She'd yearned for Dusty and Susannah to share what she and Slade had, but apparently it wasn't meant to happen.

"I think it's time for us to go home," Slade said. "I'll take Susannah and get the driver to bring the carriage around front. Why don't you round up my mother and Dusty?" He whisked Susannah into his arms and went around the outside of the hall rather than going back inside.

Several minutes passed before Isabel found Mrs. Stanfield. They went together and collected Dusty. The carriage ride home was dismal, indeed.

twelve

The following morning, Isabel was carrying a pail of milk and a pail of eggs when she finally spotted Slade riding in from the east. Quickening her pace, she rushed toward the house, handing Mrs. Stanfield the pails and hurrying back out the door. She longed to see Slade this morning, feel his arms around her, and make certain last night wasn't a dream.

She found him down by the barn, loosening Blacky's cinch so both horse and rider could eat before they headed out on another task. "Good morning!"

The expression on Slade's face stopped her midstep. "What's wrong?" Maybe she had dreamed the proposal because Slade Stanfield didn't resemble a man in love. Rather, he looked like a man with a big problem. Isabel's stomach suddenly felt sick.

"We need to talk." His grim words caused even more apprehension.

He motioned for her to sit down on an old tree stump. Since her legs were shaky, she welcomed the invitation. Running his hand down the back of his head, Slade paced a few steps away and then came back to face her. Finally, he kneeled in front of her.

"Isabel, the things I said last night—"

"You didn't mean them," she accused, jumping up and putting distance between them. Fighting tears, she stood stiff with her back to Slade.

He came to her and turned her around, raising her chin with his hand until their eyes met. "I did mean them. I meant every word. I do love you."

She swallowed hard. "But?"

"I can't marry you, Isabel."

She pulled her lips together in a tight line and closed her eyes. Her heart suddenly weighed a hundred pounds. Nodding her head, she pulled away from him, fighting the tears.

"Wait, Isabel. Please, let me explain."

She paused and looked back at him. One tear slid out, then another.

He came to her again and roughly pulled her into his arms. She laid her head against his chest, and the tears flowed unchecked. She loved him so much, and now he didn't want her, either. No one had ever wanted her, not really. Her parents loved her but always wanted to change her into her sisters. They didn't want Isabel just as she was. Neither did Slade.

"Isabel, I promised myself and God I'd not marry until Susannah did. How can I take things from life that she no longer can? Especially since I'm responsible for her condition."

Isabel raised her head to look at him. His eyes glistened with unshed tears, and the pain on his face resembled the anguish in her heart. She wanted to argue with him, but his jaw was set in determination. She'd not win.

"What about Dusty? I thought he cared about Susannah."

"Barring a miracle, he's leaving as soon as he can figure a way to take care of himself. Last night made him conclude he is in no position to care for himself, let alone another." Slade led Isabel to an oak, and they sat, leaning back against the trunk.

Isabel let out a sigh. “Does Susannah know?”

“Not yet. I think Dusty should tell her, so I’m minding my own business.” Slade swatted at a gnat.

“She might marry someone, someday. We can wait.”

“I can’t ask you to wait. What if she never marries, Isabel? You shouldn’t throw away your chance for a family on a maybe.” Slade took her hand in his. “I’ve thought about this from every angle. I don’t know what else to do except to set you free.” He squeezed her hand.

“Do you mind if I finish out my six months? Maybe in the three I have left, Susannah will meet someone else, and we won’t have to say good-bye.”

Slade kissed her hand. “There is also the matter of God.”

“God?”

“Isabel, I’m not sure exactly where you stand with Him.”

Isabel frowned. “I believe in God.”

“I know you do, but do you have a relationship with Him?”

“I talk to Him. . .occasionally.” She pulled her hand free. “If you don’t want to marry me, just say so. Don’t blame God.” Isabel jumped up and ran until she reached the house. She sneaked into her room, and lying across her bed, she let her pain pour out. Susannah must have heard the muffled sobs, for a few minutes later, she knocked softly on Isabel’s door.

“Isabel, can I come in?” she asked softly from the porch.

“Go away, Susannah. Please go away.”

Susannah ignored the request and entered. “I can’t just leave you here. Please tell me what’s wrong. How can I help?”

Isabel sat up. “Can you make your brother love me? Can you give him the desire to spend the rest of his life with me? No, I think not, so you can’t help.”

Susannah shuffled across the room and sat on the bed. In a soft voice, barely above a whisper, she said, "No more than you can make Dusty fall in love with me. No more than you can make Dusty wish to spend all his days with me." By then Susannah cried, too. "We are quite a pair, Isabel, quite a pair, indeed."

Isabel hugged Susannah. "I'm sorry. I forgot you're hurting, too."

"We are both heartbroken women heading for spinsterhood because the men we've given our hearts to don't want them," Susannah said.

Isabel laughed and cried at the same time. "Spinsterhood?"

"I don't know about you, but I will never see another man. I don't want to hurt like this again. Slade was right to keep me locked away. I should have stayed under lock and key, then I'd not hurt so much."

Isabel's hope plummeted with each of Susannah's words. There was no hope she'd marry anytime soon, which made Slade unavailable. Besides, with his new excuse, he'd probably have no interest in Isabel even if Susannah were happily married. Isabel blew out a long, slow breath. The honest truth was that Slade didn't want her. He'd acted impulsively and now regretted his actions, so he'd made up some excuse and blamed God.

Did she want to stay here anymore? She thought of Susannah, Mrs. Stanfield, Dusty, Slade, even the horses. Yes, she'd stay and finish her six months. With nowhere else to go, she'd have time to figure out where to go from here. She'd probably go home.

Lord, I'm so sorry I hurt Isabel. Please forgive me and enable her to forgive me. I thank You for bringing her into my life, even if it's only for six months. Knowing her has changed me. Loving her has changed me. Forgive me, Father, for not consulting You about my love for Isabel. Forgive me for the years of doubt and silence. Lord, my heart echoes the father in the Bible—help my unbelief. Help me to trust You. In Your Son's precious name I pray, amen.

❧

The next six weeks passed in stony silence. Isabel avoided Slade. Susannah avoided Dusty. Slade and Dusty were solemn and seldom spoke. Finally, Isabel could take no more. Even though she'd only been at the ranch for five months, she had to leave. Staying another month would be simply impossible.

"I'm riding to town today," Isabel announced to Susannah. "Would you like to come along?"

Susannah's eyes brightened. She laid her brush down on her bureau. "I don't know. What will Slade say?"

"He'll probably say no. I wasn't asking. He told me to let your mother know of any outings you and I take, so I plan to tell her after he's long gone."

Susannah grabbed her cane and moved toward Isabel. "I do want to go. I haven't ridden in such a long time." She moved her head in a defiant gesture. "I'm so tired of the miserable silence resonating through this house. For the past six weeks—ever since the Christmas ball—neither Dusty nor Slade ever say a word. You, Mama, and I carry on useless prattle, but we're only trying to cover the obvious quiet."

Isabel bobbed her head in concurrence. "I'll see you at breakfast." She, too, was sick of the silence, the brooding, and her own broken heart. Seeing Slade daily made her plight worse. That's why she'd decided to leave.

She hurried back to Susannah's room. "Please don't mention

our plans yet. Also, bring a coat. The temperature is running about sixty degrees this week." She'd miss this drier, warmer climate when she returned to San Francisco.

"All right. I'll see you in the kitchen."

After breakfast, Isabel hurried through her chores, thinking this might be one of the last days she spent with the horses. She wanted to cry but wouldn't. As soon as she finished her chores, she saddled Lady for herself and Flaxie—a small, flax-colored mare—for Susannah. Flaxie had been Susannah's horse before the accident. Then she put the other horses back in their stalls so Slade wouldn't have to later.

Isabel led both horses up to the house. Susannah waited on the front veranda, dressed in some of her old riding clothes. "I'll let your mother know we're taking a ride in a southwesterly direction." Isabel winked. "Let's get you on the horse in case she decides to come out. That way we look all ready, and she'll have fewer doubts."

Isabel took Susannah's jacket and tied it behind the saddle. "I know Slade says you always mount on the left, but today we're doing things a little differently."

Susannah laughed. "It would be hard to mount on the left with a wooden stump for the bottom half of my left leg."

"My thinking exactly."

Susannah grabbed the saddle horn and jumped, jamming her right foot into the stirrup. Isabel held on to her for support. Susannah threw her left leg over the saddle and looked like a pro in no time.

"You'll have to teach me how to do that jump. Makes you look like a cowgirl from way back." Isabel handed Susannah Flaxie's reins.

"I am a cowgirl from way back. I've been riding since I

turned three. And it feels good to be on a horse again. Thank you, Isabel."

"And thank you for accompanying me. I'll be right back."

Isabel went through the front door and straight to the kitchen. Mrs. Stanfield spent a good deal of time there each day. Grabbing two apples, she said, "Susannah and I are going for a ride." She turned to leave.

"Where, *mija?* You know Slade will want to know."

"We thought we'd head off in the direction of San Diego."

"*Si.* Don't go too far. I think rain may fall later today."

Isabel had noticed the overcast sky but hadn't thought too much about it. It rained here far less often than it did in San Francisco. "I did pack a lunch, so we will be home before supper."

Mrs. Stanfield looked worried but said nothing.

Isabel headed out the door, avoiding any other questions Mrs. Stanfield might ask.

She tossed an apple up to Susannah and mounted Lady. They rode at a leisurely pace, both chomping on their apples.

"Why are we going to San Diego?"

Isabel had dreaded this question but knew it would come sooner or later. "I plan on sending a telegram to my father, asking him to send me a ticket so I can go home."

Susannah made a disappointed clicking sound with her tongue. "Oh, Isabel, I don't want you to leave."

"I have to." Tears sprang into her eyes. "It's past time for me to go."

"Will you ever come back?" Susannah's voice resounded with disappointment and sorrow.

"No. I'll never come back." The words sounded more emotionally charged than she had intended. Her heart couldn't endure coming back. Her heart couldn't bear seeing Slade again. "But we can write." Isabel tried to sound positive, as if her leaving was a good thing, a right thing. "Maybe you can come to San Francisco one day for a visit."

"Maybe. I wish I could go with you now and get away from Dusty. I'm glad he moved out of the house and back into the bunkhouse. At least I don't have to see him every day." Susannah patted Flaxie's neck. "You know the worst part? I know he loves me. I know we could have a wonderful life, but he's too prideful and stubborn to see that. All he can see is his wheelchair."

"Your brother's not much different. He told me he loves me, but he can't marry me because of God. I think it takes a lot of nerve to blame God. A lot of nerve."

Susannah got real quiet. Finally she asked, "Isabel, tell me about your relationship with God."

"Why do you and Slade keep speaking of a *relationship*—just like my parents used to? How do you have a relationship with an invisible God?"

"That's the amazing part." Excitement filled Susannah's tone. "The God of the entire universe, the maker of heaven and earth yearns to have a relationship with each one of us." Susannah held up her index finger. "The first step is realizing you are a sinner in need of a Savior."

"But I'm not that bad. I've never murdered anybody or anything."

"Have you ever lied?"

Guilt stabbed Isabel's heart as she remembered misleading Mrs. Stanfield just that morning.

"Or cheated or treated somebody badly?"

More memories surfaced. She'd treated her own sister

pretty badly when she wanted Chandler for herself and he chose Magdalene. Isabel nodded, hoping Susannah wouldn't think less of her because she'd done a few rotten things.

"To a holy God, sin is sin. It doesn't have to be murder or stealing. Even something as seemingly innocent as gossip is very offensive to Him."

Gossip—add another transgression to her list. She and Josephine, a friend from back home, had not only gossiped about Magdalene, they had slandered her. Isabel felt warm. All this soul-searching brought a nauseous feeling over her. "You're right. I am a sinner."

"And the wages of sin is death," Susannah spoke softly, reverently.

"But the gift of God is eternal life through Christ Jesus our Lord." Isabel finished the verse for her. "My father taught me that as a little girl. Only today, it somehow makes more sense than ever before."

Susannah looked like she might cry. "I'm glad, Isabel."

"So how does one make Christ her Savior?"

Susannah grinned an ear-to-ear, my-oh-my-am-I-happy kind of grin. "It's easy. You ask. You admit to Him you've sinned, even name the ones that come to mind. Then, you ask forgiveness for your sins. Invite Jesus to come into your life as your Lord and Savior. That's when the relationship starts."

"And what happens if I never ask?"

Susannah's face took on a serious, frightened look. "Upon your death, you are sent to hell because you didn't accept Christ's love and payment for your sins. He died on the cross in your place, but you must accept the gift."

"By inviting Him to forgive me and come into my life?" Isabel wanted to be certain she understood.

"Exactly! Then you get a relationship with God, and you get to spend eternity with Him in heaven."

"Instead of hell without Him?"

"Do you want to do that, Isabel—invite God into your heart and life?"

Her pulse raced, and she knew now was the time. She licked her suddenly dry lips. "I do." The girls stopped their horses side by side. Susannah reached for Isabel's hand. "Do you want me to help you?"

Isabel smiled at Susannah, loving her all the more. "No. I think I understand." She closed her eyes and bowed her head. "Lord God, it's me, Isabel. After all these years, what my father has said about You makes sense. I am a sinner." Emotion choked her words. "And You are the Savior, so today I ask You to come. . . ." Isabel swallowed hard and wiped tears from her cheeks. "Come and forgive me. Come and save me. Come have a relationship with me." Isabel felt warmth and peace wash over her. "I thank You in Jesus' name, Amen."

Both she and Susannah cried happy tears. "Now you and I will spend eternity together, Isabel, even if we never see each other again on this earth. Maybe my mansion will even be next to yours."

"My own mansion? I've heard about that but never personalized the thought before." Isabel smiled.

"On streets of gold."

What more could she want? "Speaking of streets. . ." Isabel stopped Lady on the outskirts of town. "Do you know the way to the telegraph office?"

Susannah said, "Follow me."

A couple of turns and they were there. Susannah waited with the horses while Isabel went inside. Susannah didn't want to make a spectacle of herself getting off and on Flaxie. She also loaned Isabel the money to pay for the telegram.

Isabel dictated her message to the worker. "Want to come home. Stop. Please send a train ticket. Stop. In care of Slade Stanfield San Diego, California. Stop. Accepted Christ today. Stop. Love and miss you. Stop. Isabel." She paid the man. The thought of leaving Slade, Susannah, the ranch—all the people and things she'd grown to love—broke her heart. "But for him, I know it's best," she whispered on her way out the door.

"We'd better hurry, Isabel. The sky toward the ranch looks dark."

Isabel jumped on Lady. "Let's go," she hollered. The wind had picked up and lifted her hat off her head. She chased it down the street, finally retrieving it. She might need it to keep the rain off her head. Pushing the hat down low, she remounted Lady. They took off in a gallop toward the ranch.

❧

"I think it's going to rain," Slade said to Dusty, staring up at the sky. "Maybe we should call it a day and get back early."

Dusty sniffed. "Yeah, smells like rain for certain."

"Thanks for helping me with the fencing today. Having you riding Buck and stretching the wire was a huge time saver," Slade commented as he gathered up his tools and packed them in his saddlebags.

"It's the least I can do. Feels good to get out of the bunkhouse and do something useful."

Slade mounted Blacky. He'd hoped his plan to help Dusty feel needed wouldn't backfire, and it hadn't. "Have you been following Doc's orders and exercising your legs every day?" he asked.

"Yeah. My legs are getting a little stronger each day, but they still won't hold me up. I don't know how Susannah does it. The crutches rub sores under my arms, but I guess even sores beat riding around in a wheelchair."

Big wet drops fell from the sky. "We'd better hurry, or we'll be soaked. Can you gallop?"

Dusty nodded, and both men set out in a gallop toward home. Slade hopped off his horse and opened the barn door. Dusty rode through, and Slade led Blacky in. The drops falling on the roof made a loud, thudding noise.

"That's some downpour," Slade commented, helping Dusty off his mount and handing him his crutches.

While Dusty rubbed down his horse, Slade took the saddle and carried it over to the rack. He prayed today would go a long way in building Dusty's belief and confidence that he was still a capable cowhand.

As Slade led Dusty's gelding to his stall, he noticed Lady was missing from hers. "Flaxie is missing, too."

"What?" Dusty asked from the front of the barn where he was rubbing down Blacky.

"Lady and Flaxie are missing." Slade felt panic rising up from his stomach. "You wait here. I'm going to run to the house. I'll be back."

Slade ran as fast as his legs would carry him and was still soaked to the bone when he reached the house. He opened the front door and yelled, not wanting to track water and mud all over. "Mama."

Her worried face confirmed his suspicions even before she said anything. "*Mijo,* are the girls back?"

Slade shook his head. "Where did they go?"

"For a ride—toward town."

Slade shook his head. Did he go look for them or hope they were safe? He'd never been patient at waiting. "I'll go search for them."

"Be careful. I'll pray, *mijo.*"

He kissed Mama's cheek.

"Wait. I'll grab coats and blankets."

"I'll stop for them on my way out." Slade ran back to the barn.

thirteen

"You can't go out in this," Dusty yelled above the rain pelting the roof.

"I have to. I can't risk leaving them out there in this." Slade grabbed Blacky's bridle and headed to his stall.

"Then I'm going with you." Dusty hobbled behind him with Buck's bridle.

Slade wanted to say no, but the man had been stripped of so much of his dignity the past few months, all Slade could do was nod in agreement. Slade carried Dusty's saddle to him and they hurried to get their horses ready. "Just when I'm finally convinced Isabel has been right all along, this happens," Slade yelled as he tightened his cinch.

"Right about what?"

"Susannah deserving a normal life. I give her a little freedom, and look what happens." Slade helped Dusty into his saddle and opened the barn door, and they rode out into the pouring rain.

Mama stood on the veranda with coats and blankets. Slade shoved the blankets into his saddlebags, grabbed a coat for himself, and handed one to Dusty.

"I imagine they took the main road. We'll have to take it slow. This mud is slick."

Dusty kept his head ducked against the rain, but he gave Slade a quick nod.

Rain dripped into Slade's eyes and slammed against his face, but he'd not give up until he found the girls.

God, is this Your way of teaching me to trust You? He thought back to his request a few weeks ago that God heal his unbelief. Was this some sort of test?

"In the four years I've been here, I've never seen it rain like this." Dusty shouted to be heard.

"Me, either." That worried him. How long until the normally dry gullies filled with water and ran out over the road, making continuing impossible?

Lord, please hold Susannah and Isabel in Your righteous right hand. Please keep them safe. I admit only You can provide safety and protection. Though I thought I could keep Susannah out of harm's way, I now know that job belongs to You, not me. Forgive me for trying to take Your role in my sister's life.

Again, I ask You to forgive my three years of anger. I surrender my future, Susannah's future, and Isabel's future to You—the God of the universe. Please use this to draw Isabel to You. I ask for their safety in Jesus' name, amen.

Peace settled on Slade. He knew whatever happened, God was in control.

At the bottom of the hill, a wash filled with water ran across the road, wiping the roadbed away.

"It looks deep," Dusty commented.

Slade didn't want to believe it was, so he dismounted and used a tree branch to gauge. The water was several feet deep and ran at quite a pace. Slade knew it would be foolish to attempt to cross. They might end up stuck out in the weather for days.

Trust, his heart kept saying. He bowed his head. *I'm helpless, Lord. I trust You to work Your good and perfect will in this situation.*

"We'll have to go back. No use us being stranded, too." Slade hopped on Blacky and they returned to the ranch.

"I'm dropping you at the house. This mud is too slick for you and your crutches. I'll take the horses down."

Once in the barn, Slade dropped to his knees and prayed again.

Mama had hot bowls of soup ready when Slade finally returned to the house. He changed into dry clothes and joined Dusty at the table.

"I must speak with both of you," she informed Slade and Dusty. "I have watched you both destroy the love you have for Susannah and Isabel."

Slade glanced at Dusty. He looked as guilty as Slade felt.

"I say nothing. Now I must speak. Love is a gift. How will you feel if they don't come back alive?" Mama stood at the end of the table, her arms crossed.

"Devastated," Slade answered.

"You both let your male pride get in the way. Do you love Susannah?" she asked Dusty.

"I do." His quiet voice was self-condemning.

"Then why are you not married? Or at least courting? Because of a few rude men and a bruised ego, you walk away from this good and perfect gift from God's hand?" Mama shook her head in disapproval.

Dusty cleared his throat. "I have no way to provide for her, no way to protect her. Both of those responsibilities are given to a man with regard to his wife and family, by God Himself."

"When you marry Susannah, we become your family. Families look out for each other and fight battles together. We would help until you are well enough to take over."

Dusty hung his head. "I have nothing to offer her, no home, no possessions—nothing."

"And if she never returns, will that still matter? What will your regrets be?"

Slade felt for Dusty and knew his own reckoning with his mama was coming.

Dusty raised his gaze and met Mama's reproachful look. "I'll regret hurting her, driving her away, and not making her my wife."

"*Si.*" Mama wore a satisfied expression on her face. "And you, Slade—"

"I told you I'd not marry until Susannah did." He wouldn't let her run over him the way she'd just done to Dusty.

"That is now taken care of."

"And I'm not sure about Isabel's relationship with God."

"Did you ask her?" Mama drew her brows together.

"She believes but doesn't understand the relationship part."

"She will soon. I've been praying."

Slade envied his mother's faith.

"If anything happens to either of them, both Dusty and I will be heartsick. Isabel is as important to me as Susannah." He smiled. "I'm taken with her, and yes, I have told her I love her."

"And you know, in spite of this disaster, she is correct?"

"Yes, Mama, I know. I've already repented. I had no right to keep Susannah locked up these three years. I just pray I'll have the chance to tell her how sorry I am." Slade stared at his soup, which had long since cooled.

"Because her leg is missing doesn't mean she can't live a normal life just like you and me."

Slade nodded. "I promised God at the first opportunity, I'll make things right with Susannah."

"And never interfere in her life again?" Mama stared straight into his soul.

"Never."

"Since we have this worked out, you may both eat now." Mama moved toward the kitchen. "Don't forget to pray."

❧

The girls galloped for a little ways, but soon rain pelted them in the face, and they had to slow down. The rain fell harder, and soon they were soaked. Isabel shivered.

"We have to get out of this. We'll end up with pneumonia," Susannah shouted over the deafening roar of the wind and rain. "There's an old shack along here somewhere, if nobody tore it down. Pray, Isabel. Pray we'll find it."

Isabel searched the horizon but didn't see a shack. They rode awhile longer, taking turns praying aloud and begging God to provide a way out.

"There it is!" Susannah hollered and pointed northeast. They rode toward the rundown hut. "I hope that it's still abandoned."

"Sure looks it." If not for the storm, Isabel wouldn't take money to enter the old shack. She climbed down and opened the door. Her hand quivered with fear at what she might find inside or what might find her. She returned to Susannah a minute later. "Since it doesn't have a porch, and the floors are dirt, let's take the horses in with us."

"A horse in the house?"

Isabel chuckled at the thought, feeling much better now that they'd found cover. She led Lady inside. Susannah waited just outside the door. Isabel helped her dismount and led Flaxie in. Susannah held on to the wall and hobbled in on her own. Isabel tended the horses, and Susannah checked out the two rooms.

"Someone must use this place occasionally and keep it stocked. There's wood in the fireplace all ready to burn and canned goods in the cupboard."

Isabel wanted to cry with joy. "Thank You, Lord. Now we can warm up and dry out our clothes." She placed the saddles in the corner and laid the saddle blankets out in the other room so they could dry out of the way. By the time Isabel was done, Susannah had a fire going in the fireplace.

Both girls huddled on the floor in front of the blaze. Isabel began to warm from the outside in. "You said earlier that the first step to a relationship with God was inviting Christ into my life. What comes next?"

"That is the only thing required for forgiveness and eternity, but the Bible says we need to get baptized. It's a public declaration of our new life in Christ and follows right after salvation. But to know God like you know a friend, you talk to Him daily through prayer and you listen to Him daily by reading His Word."

"Do all Christians do that?"

"No. Some only think about God on Sunday, but He wants to be closer to us than that. He wants us to come to Him every day."

"I hope I'll do what He wants." Isabel walked to the window. "The rain has let up a little. I'm going to the shed beside the house. Maybe more firewood is stored in there."

"Be careful."

"I will." Isabel opened the door and ran out into the rain. She'd almost dried out, and now she'd be soaked again. She ran to the shed and tugged on the door. After three tries, it finally opened. Not only were there piles of wood, there was a pile of hay. She made several trips back and forth, carrying armloads of wood and then armloads of hay. She didn't plan to go back outside anytime soon, so she brought in enough for at least the next day. While she took care of this, Susannah opened jars of canned peaches for them. Isabel was so hungry that she'd have eaten just about anything. Well, not anything.

"Why do you think this place is here and so well stocked?"

"I remember Slade said this little place used to be the main house on a small ranch. When the couple grew too old to manage it, a neighboring ranch bought them out. That happens a lot out here. The Ochoa place is at least twice its original size. Anyway, if I have the story straight, this is now part of the biggest ranch in the area. They most likely use this when they are out mending fences."

"And get caught in the rain." Isabel laughed. "In spite of it all, I feel wonderful. I feel lucky—"

"Not luck, Isabel, but God."

Isabel smiled. She had a lot to learn. "All right, I feel God, not luck, took care of us, and somehow I feel lighter than I have in years."

Susannah hugged her. "You're glowing. You won't have to tell anyone what happened; they'll know just by looking."

❧

Two days later, the rains had stopped, but the creeks all ran high. Slade couldn't wait any longer. He'd take his chances with the water, but he couldn't chance Susannah and Isabel dying while they waited for him.

He and Dusty rode to the Ochoas'. Several men volunteered to help in the search. Slade mapped out a plan and assigned each man a few square miles. "Look under every rock. Check every possibility. Don't stop until you've searched every inch of your area." Slade handed each pair of men their map.

He and Dusty kept to the road and the areas running along each side. They'd burned most of their daylight hours. Dusk fell.

"Slade, I see smoke." He pointed at the hut.

Hope rose. Slade squeezed Blacky with his legs, and the

horse broke into a canter. "Anybody could have found cover in that shack. Let's just pray it's them."

The door flew open before he dismounted. Isabel ran to him. He jumped off his horse and Isabel landed in his arms. "Slade," she sobbed and held on to him with all her might.

He kissed the top of her head and held her just as tight.

Out of the corner of his eye, he watched Dusty use his arm strength and lower himself to the ground right at the front door. He grabbed the door for support. Susannah stood in the doorway, tears streaking down her face. Dusty reached for her. She fell into his arms. He kissed her cheeks, her lips, her forehead.

Isabel turned, and together she and Slade watched the event unfold.

"I love you, Susannah. I need you. Please say you'll be my wife."

Susannah wrapped her arms around his neck. "Just try to get rid of me."

Dusty wiped her tears away with his thumbs, and then he bent his head for one very long kiss.

Isabel blushed. "Slade, I'm sorry. You were right all along. Susannah doesn't need adventure. She needs safety. I promised God I'd quit meddling in your family."

"You promised God?" Slade barely dared to breathe, waiting for Isabel's answer.

Isabel's smile shamed the sun. "I now have a relationship with Jesus. I asked Him to come into my life as my Lord and Savior."

"Oh, Isabel." He pulled her back into his embrace, his heart overflowing with joy. God had removed all the obstacles.

"Slade?"

"Mmm?" He never wanted to quit holding her.

"Can you forgive me? I mean truly forgive me."

"Of course I can, Isabel." He pulled back and gazed into her eyes.

"I do have good news for you."

He smiled. "More good news?"

"I'm going home."

His heart felt like it dropped out of his chest. "To San Francisco?"

"It's time. I need to make things right with my family. I figured you'd be thrilled. Now you can run your sister's life any way you want."

"I'll miss you." His heart already hurt.

"And I'll miss all of you. You've become like a second family to me."

He noticed she lumped him in with the rest of the family. Isabel must have realized she wasn't in love with him after all. He'd lost her, and he had no one to blame but himself.

"Guess we should start home." Slade didn't wish to talk more about her leaving. "Where are the horses?"

Isabel giggled. "In the house."

Slade shook his head. With Isabel, one never knew. Ah, but he knew—knew he loved her, knew he'd miss her, knew his heart would never heal. But she seemed sure of her plans. He'd not try to convince her to stay. He'd respect her decision, even if it killed him inside.

"Isabel, will you forgive me for hurting you and for not listening more readily to your suggestions about Susannah?"

"I do, and you're forgiven." Her eyes were serene, and he knew she'd found peace.

When they walked into the cabin, Dusty and Susannah were still kissing. Slade cleared his throat, and they both looked over at him.

Slade picked up his baby sister and twirled her around.

"I'm getting married," she declared.

"I know." Slade grinned. "I've spent a lot of time with this fellow the past few days. He's in love with you."

Susannah gazed at Dusty. "And I with him."

"Before we leave, I want you to know how sorry I am for holding you prisoner these past few years." He hugged Susannah tight.

"I know you did it because you love me and wanted to protect me."

"Now you have someone else to protect you, so I'll stay out of your life." He kissed her cheek. "Let's head for Rancho San Miguel. I know one mother who'll be glad to see you both."

fourteen

They stopped by the Ochoa ranch on the way home. Mr. Ochoa fired off his gun three times to signal the men to stop the search. Then he led them inside, offering tea or coffee. After all Mr. Ochoa had done to help Slade, Isabel knew Slade felt obligated to visit, so the four of them sat in the parlor, sipping tea with Mr. Ochoa.

"I sent a man to town today." Mr. Ochoa opened the newspaper dated Thursday, February 7, 1884. "Most severe wind and rain storm ever seen in San Diego," he read. Looking up over the paper and the top of his spectacles, he said, "You girls are lucky to be alive."

"Not luck, sir," Isabel stated.

"God," she and Susannah said in unison and then giggled.

He frowned and continued reading. "The town has suffered considerable damage, especially the railroad."

"The railroad?" He'd caught Isabel's interest.

"Washouts are reported, and at least one bridge is gone."

Isabel's heart sank. *How will I get home?*

"Many roads are gone, as well, and the telegraph lines are down."

Isabel's eyes burned. Her father might never have received her telegram.

"Seems it will take months before everything is repaired and up and working again."

Months? Isabel glanced at Slade. He watched her. How could she stay here for months? She had to get away; her heart couldn't take much more.

"Isabel, you don't look well. Perhaps we should get you home." Slade rose. "Thank you for all your kindness and hospitality, sir. We most appreciate it, but we need to get these ladies home and rested up."

Mr. Ochoa escorted them out and bid them good day.

Dusty and Susannah talked the entire ride home, so Isabel was able to be quiet. *Now what, God? Please get me out of here.* She almost felt like she'd smother if she couldn't get away.

"Isabel." Slade rode up next to Lady. "You appeared quite upset by the news, especially regarding the railroad and telegraph lines."

She stared off at the horizon, not wanting to look into his face, the face she loved. "I sent my father a telegram on Tuesday, requesting he send me a ticket home." She chewed on her bottom lip, fighting the desire to give in to fatigue and disappointment. "Now, I don't know if he received my note, but even if he did, the tracks won't be passable for several months." Her words cracked with emotion.

"You want to go home really badly, don't you?" His tone carried sadness, but she'd not think about that or hope his feelings might have changed. He didn't want her. He'd made that much clear to her on more than one occasion.

"I do. I'd leave tomorrow if I could." She blinked, fighting the impending tears.

"What about Susannah's wedding? I know she'd like you here for that."

A wedding was the last thing Isabel wished to attend. "Well, she'll probably get her desire since the train isn't running." She almost sounded bitter.

Slade didn't say anything, and they rode the rest of the way in silence.

They stopped at the house first. Mrs. Stanfield cried and hugged them all about ten times each.

"Dusty and Susannah wish to speak to you in private, Mama, so Isabel and I will take the horses down to the barn." Slade led two of the mounts, and Isabel led the other two. "You look weary. Why don't you let me take care of them, and you can return to the house for some rest?"

"I don't wish to interrupt your mother, Susânnah, and Dusty. Besides, I enjoy spending time with Lady."

Slade accepted her answer. He finished unsaddling the other three and gave each horse a good rubdown. She did the same with Lady, only she felt like she moved in slow motion. She'd gotten little sleep either night and now felt tired beyond words.

They left the barn together. "Isabel, if you're really in such a hurry to go home, I'll buy you a ticket on a stage."

She stopped and burst into tears, covering her face with her hands.

Slade took her into his arms. "Are you sure you want to leave?"

"You have no idea how much." She laid her head against his chest and listened to the steady beat of his heart. *I have to get away from you, Slade. I have to escape. My heart is broken into a million pieces and needs time to heal.*

For several minutes, Slade held her. For several minutes, she reveled in his touch. "I'll take you tomorrow to catch the stage." His voice was low and controlled.

"Thank you."

❧

Slade ached to kiss her, but he wouldn't. Instead, he'd hold her as long as she needed.

I love you, Isabel. How am I ever going to let you go? What happened to my plan to ask for your hand in marriage?

He knew what had happened. Her announcement that she was going home happened. The words not only left him stunned and silent, but they also sent his heart reeling in pain.

Finally, Isabel pulled out of his embrace and wiped her tears with her palms. If only she knew how dirty her face was. All she did was rearrange the grime. Even so, she was beautiful to him. He wanted to memorize each feature so he'd never forget that face—her eyes, her smile, her dimples.

When they arrived at the house, Isabel said, "I think I'd love to rest. Will you excuse me?"

Slade proceeded to the kitchen, certain his mother and sister sat around the worktable planning a wedding. They didn't disappoint him.

"Where's Isabel?" his mother asked.

He explained.

"Will we have another family wedding soon?" Susannah asked.

Slade wondered if he could say the words aloud without giving away the depth of his pain. "Isabel is returning to San Francisco tomorrow."

They stared at him. He walked away before they could probe. The only day in his life Slade remembered feeling this bad was the day his father died. Today, his and Isabel's future died. She'd never be his wife, never bear his children. And he'd never hold her again.

❧

Slade went to the barn in the predawn hours the next morning so he and Isabel could get an early start. The sun had just begun to lighten the sky. As soon as he opened the door, he heard a strange sound. He followed the noise, discovering

Isabel sobbing into Lady's neck. Did he stay? Did he go?

Frozen in indecision, he heard her say, "I'm so sad to leave you. You have no idea how much I'll miss you."

She'd miss a horse but not him? For some reason, that really bothered him. He turned to slip away unnoticed when he heard Isabel call to him.

"Slade." She wiped her eyes with the sleeve of her shirt. "I was telling Lady good-bye."

"I'm sorry. I didn't mean to interrupt."

She glanced back at Lady. "Do you mind if I go ahead and do the chores one last time?" She sounded as if she'd really miss her routine.

"Not if you really want to." He shrugged.

"I do. I love this ranch and all the little jobs that come with it." They walked together to the straw shed. "I grew up in the city, and we never had animals. I had no idea how much I'd grow to love them."

Then stay, Isabel. Stay. Slade's gaze rose to the sky. "Maybe you should marry a man with some land so you can have animals of your own."

"Maybe I should." She grabbed the pitchfork.

"Do you want me to milk Daisy and collect the eggs?"

Her eyes glistened with extra moisture. She shook her head. "No." She smiled slightly. "You must think I'm silly, but I want to do it all one last time."

"No, not silly, just sentimental." He touched her cheek. "I'll get the buckboard ready."

"Wait. Would you mind if we rode the horses instead?"

"Not if that's what you want. As soon as Blacky and Lady finish eating, I'll saddle them while you finish your chores."

"Thank you." She rose up on tiptoe and kissed his cheek. "For everything. You're almost like the brother I never had."

Brother? He certainly didn't consider her a sister. No, there was nothing brotherly about the feelings he had for Isabel. Nothing brotherly at all.

Slade went back up to the house. Susannah met him at the door. "I can't find Isabel."

"She's down at the barn doing her chores." At Susannah's disapproving expression, Slade said, "She wanted to. Not my idea or suggestion. I went down to do them myself, but she insisted she had to do them one last time."

Susannah shook her head. "What does that tell you?"

Slade lifted his brows, not certain what it told him. "That she likes caring for animals?"

Susannah sighed in exasperation. "No. She doesn't want to leave."

"She doesn't?"

"Of course not." Susannah put her hand on her hip; the other held her cane.

"Susannah, I asked her if she was certain she wanted to leave. She said yes. Not maybe. Not sort of, but yes!"

"Did you ask her to stay?" Mama questioned from the doorway.

"No! She can't wait to get home. Almost panicked when she thought she might be stuck here a few months." His voice rose both in pitch and in volume. "Don't you understand? She can't wait to get away from me."

There. He'd stated the truth. Isabel Fairchild loved the ranch, the animals, even the chores. She loved Mama, Susannah, even Dusty. He was the one she didn't love.

Slade strode to the barn. He planned on saddling the horses and waiting outside until Isabel was ready to leave. He refused to take any more badgering questions from those two women!

❧

Isabel took her time feeding each horse, rubbing their noses, talking to them. She cried a few tears, too, but tried to leave each one with a positive memory of her. Then she milked Daisy, carrying on a conversation with her all the while. She talked to each hen while collecting eggs. Then she carried the milk and eggs to the house.

She went around back and into the kitchen, hoping she'd not run into anyone. She didn't want Mrs. Stanfield or Susannah asking too many questions. Slade's raised voice carried to her. *Why is he so angry?* She froze and listened.

"No! She can't wait to get home. Almost panicked when she thought she might be stuck here a few months." His voice rose both in pitch and in volume. "Don't you understand? She can't wait to get away from me."

Isabel felt like Slade had punched her. Is that what he thought? She slipped out the back door and ran through the grove of trees to the barn and into Lady's stall. Out of breath, she asked the mare, "What should I do?"

In a sense, Slade was right. She was leaving because of him. Every word he said was true, but not because she hated him. She loved him. "I'll just let him believe the worst." She put Lady's halter on and led the horse to the hitching rail. "I don't want him to know I'm pining."

One by one, Isabel led the horses to the pasture while she cleaned their stalls. After cleaning the water troughs and laying fresh straw, she returned to the pasture to watch them. Slade already had both horses saddled and was fixing a gate.

"I'll go say my good-byes, and we can leave."

He nodded but didn't follow her. She knocked on the bunkhouse door. Dusty stepped out onto the porch, relying very little on his crutches.

"I like seeing you standing on your own two feet." She smiled.

"Me, too. I think I'll make an almost complete recovery." His eyes probed her face.

"No more buggy racing."

Dusty laughed. "I'm not planning on any, and I fear my bride would have my hide."

Isabel giggled along with him. Then she got serious. "You take care of her."

Dusty nodded. "And you take care of yourself." He pulled her into a tight hug. "I'll miss you, Isabel. You kind of turned this place upside down for a while."

The tears were coming, and Isabel didn't want to cry. She dug for strength. She leaned up and kissed his cheek. "I'll remember you always." Turning away quickly, she strode toward the house.

She heard Dusty say, "And I'll remember you."

But she didn't turn or acknowledge his words. Instead, she took deep breaths and whispered, "I will not cry. I will not cry. I will not cry."

Finding Mrs. Stanfield in the kitchen, she gave the woman a quick hug, hoping to avoid any questions or an emotional scene. After the hug, Mrs. Stanfield put her hands on Isabel's shoulders. "Many thanks, *mija.*" She kissed each cheek. Isabel noticed the tears in her eyes.

"Many thanks to you. My stay with your family was lovely. I will never forget you." Isabel wiped away a couple of determined tears. No matter how fast she blinked, they insisted on escaping.

She found Susannah in the garden on her knees, getting the soil ready for spring planting. "Thanks to you I am now allowed to play in the dirt."

They both laughed.

Susannah struggled to stand up. Isabel reached down to help her.

"No, let me do it. Tomorrow you won't be here to help, so I need to do this by myself."

Isabel took a step back to give her room. After four tries, Susannah managed to stand and get her cane situated. With a dirt smudge on her cheek and dirt under her fingernails, she was quite the sight.

"I wish you'd stay."

"I can't. I have a deal to make with you, though. I'll trade you this riding outfit for my traveling suit you liked so much."

Susannah's face lit up.

"You'll need to have it altered. I'm sure it's too long for you, but I won't be needing it."

Susannah nodded and looked toward the barn. "Isabel," she choked out.

"Let's not cry." Isabel blinked back more tears. "I know how you feel, and you know how I feel."

Susannah wasn't very good at this. Her face puckered up, and the tears ran freely down her cheeks. "I can't help it. I'm losing a friend and the only sister I've ever had."

Isabel lost her battle with the tears. She hugged Susannah. "I will miss you. You are so dear to me. Please write to me and tell me of your life."

"And you write and tell me of yours."

Just don't tell me of Slade's. I won't be able to bear the news when he someday marries another. Isabel stepped back. "I must go. Will you take Lady carrots every now and again? She's come to expect them."

Susannah nodded, her nose red and her face blotchy. Isabel walked a few steps away and then ran back. "I love you,

Susannah." She hugged her tight again and then ran toward Slade and the horses.

❧

Slade watched Isabel in the garden with Susannah. He couldn't hear what they said, but the scene played out painfully before him. He knew they both cried, and he nearly cried along with them. He was ready for this day to be over, not that he desired Isabel to leave, but he was ready for his heart to start healing.

Isabel stopped halfway between the garden and the barn. He busied himself with the horses, keeping one eye on her. She removed a lace hanky from her pocket and wiped the moisture from her cheeks and eyes. Raising her chin, she sauntered the rest of the way to the barn.

"I'm ready." Her voice was composed and calm. He handed her Lady's reins, and Isabel mounted. He hopped on Blacky, and they rode past the house and toward the road. Isabel sat ramrod straight, and he knew she tried not to look at Susannah on the veranda, crying in Dusty's arms, and she tried not to look at Mama waving her good-bye next to them. She almost made it but then gave in and turned to wave.

Slade gave her a few minutes of quiet to compose herself. Then he asked, "What are your plans when you get back to San Francisco?"

She chuckled. "I owe a lot of people apologies. I guess I'll start with those."

Slade admired the changes in Isabel. She'd grown into a woman of integrity. "And then?"

She stared into his eyes for several seconds. "And then. . .I don't know."

She had no plans, yet such an urgency to get home. Another reason to believe she couldn't stand him. "Will you marry Horace A. Peabody?"

"I'm surprised you remembered. No, I don't think I'll ever marry. Paul says it's good to be single."

She was quoting Scripture! "But you once said yes to my proposal."

He glimpsed pain on her face for one brief moment. "That was before I put God in charge of my life. Now I have to do what He says, so it's a good thing you changed your mind. We'd have both made a huge mistake."

Her words cut into his heart. *It's a good thing you changed your mind.* But he'd changed his mind for reasons that no longer existed. If only he hadn't run ahead of God in the first place, he wouldn't be in this predicament now. He'd be asking for the first time, and maybe, just maybe, she'd have said yes.

We'd have both made a huge mistake. How did she go from loving him to considering him a huge mistake? He rubbed the back of his neck, realizing he'd never understand God's fairer creatures. And knowing he yearned to understand Isabel and discover what went wrong between them.

fifteen

Suddenly, the events of Christmas night popped into Slade's mind. He'd been on the balcony with Isabel during the ball, staring into her mesmerizing emerald eyes. *"I realize now you were a godsend. We all needed you, Isabel, but me even more than Susannah. I'm so grateful for everything you've done for her benefit."*

He'd touched her deeply. He knew at that moment he never wanted her to leave. Then he'd kissed her, tenderly holding her face in his hands. *"I love you, Isabel."*

He smiled, remembering her shocked expression. *"You do?"* she'd asked.

"I do," he'd assured her. Then he'd blurted out a proposal. Without thinking, without praying.

Isabel's mouth had dropped open. *"Oh, Slade, yes! A million times, yes!"*

Almost immediately, he'd known he'd made a grave error. The next morning he'd attempted to right his wrong. He recalled the apprehension in her expression. *"Isabel, the things I said last night—"*

"You didn't mean them," she'd accused.

"I did mean them. I meant every word. I do love you." And he had—still did, for that matter. He'd not lied, but he had failed to consult the Lord.

Then he'd uttered the words that brought pain to her face and tears to her eyes. *"I can't marry you, Isabel."* When she'd turned to leave, he'd tried explaining, talking his way out, but looking back, each word condemned him more. No wonder Isabel had wanted to leave as soon as possible.

When he'd reminded her of his promise to God to not marry until Susannah was married, Isabel had been so understanding, even offering to wait. She had been willing to wait for him no matter how long it took, and now she couldn't wait to get away from him. One of life's ironies.

He'd informed her that he couldn't ask her to wait. But on reflection, he realized he had sounded like a man with too many excuses, a man who didn't really love her. They'd barely spoken since.

And I wonder why the girl desperately wants to escape me? Thinking back, I want to escape me.

The seriousness of sin struck Slade's heart. Sin didn't simply hurt the one sinning; it also affected everyone that person loved. Because Slade had not sought God first, Isabel had been deeply hurt. The consequences of sin were far reaching. Not only had Isabel been affected, but he'd also ruined their chance for a future because now she could barely stand him.

Lord, I'm so sorry. I'm so sorry. The weight of his sorrow was breaking his heart.

❧

Much to Isabel's relief, Slade had finally quit talking, but his brooding silence drove her to distraction. Besides, conversation kept her from thinking, and she'd rather not think. "This is beautiful country, isn't it?"

Surprise etched itself on Slade's face. "None prettier."

"I love southern California. I'd not know that if I'd made it to Arizona. Guess I owe Mr. Tripp a debt of gratitude." She laughed at such an absurd notion.

"But you missed your great dance-hall adventure," Slade reminded her.

Isabel scanned the hills and valleys. "I think in response to my father's pleas, God intervened and gave me a different adventure."

"You enjoyed ranch life, didn't you?"

Isabel smiled at him. "I can't begin to tell you how much. You and Susannah are so lucky—" She quickly changed her word choice. "So blessed to have this legacy."

"What about you, Isabel? What's your legacy?"

She thought about his question before giving an answer. "My legacy is a father and mother who love the Lord. Father gave up a career in banking to become a fisherman because he and my mother saw the effect money and high society were having on their three daughters. They made a huge sacrifice for our sakes."

"That's a rich legacy. And in a few days, you'll be home."

"That I will." She felt some apprehension. She'd never fit in well before. Why did she think she would now? *I'm not going there to fit in. I'm leaving to get away from Slade.*

"You don't seem very excited to be going home," Slade commented.

"I'll be happy to see my family again and make things right with them, but I'll miss all of you and Lady."

Slade stopped his horse. "We're here," he said quietly.

She hadn't noticed, but they'd reached the stage depot. Her throat grew tight. She pulled her lips together, hoping they'd dam the emotions welling within. This was it. Good-bye. She'd never be in this city or be with Slade again.

He dismounted and handed her Blacky's reins. "I'll go purchase your ticket."

She nodded, gazing in each direction to imprint this place forever in her heart.

❧

Slade stood in line and bought the ticket. He swallowed, then swallowed again, trying to dislodge the lump threatening to choke him. Stopping at the edge of the street, he studied Isabel. She'd gotten off her horse and nuzzled Lady's nose. He couldn't see her face but was fairly certain the tears fell. She kissed the small star on Lady's head, and Slade wished leaving him were as difficult.

He cleared his throat and handed Isabel her ticket. "We were almost late. They are ready to board now, so you need to get in that line." He pointed to several people with bags and tickets. Handing her an envelope, he said, "This is for you."

She opened it, saw the money inside, and started to protest.

"You earned every cent." He closed her hand around the envelope. The contact brought a stronger ache inside him. "And you'll need money to eat along the road."

"Thank you, Slade." She kissed his cheek and ran for the line.

Slade touched his face, still feeling the imprint of her lips. Absently rubbing Lady's nose, he watched Isabel. Her head was bent forward, and she kept wiping her face with her lace handkerchief. *Lord, please get her safely home.* He'd wait here until she boarded.

The stage driver opened the door, and one by one the line of people were swallowed up into the coach. Soon Isabel, too, would be out of sight.

Ask her to stay. Slade couldn't rid himself of the impression. *Ask her to stay.* He tied Lady and Blacky to a nearby hitching post and ran the short distance. He stopped a few feet from the coach. Isabel had just handed her ticket to the driver.

"Don't leave."

She paused, her foot on the first step.

"Isabel, please don't leave."

She turned. Their eyes met. He saw the hesitation on her face.

"I love you."

Biting her bottom lip and with fear in her eyes, she stared at him.

He moved toward her, taking her hand in his. He led her a few steps away from the stage. "I can't imagine my life without you in it."

She didn't trust him not to change his mind again. He could see it in the battle of emotions warring on her face.

"I'm sorry. I know I hurt you so deeply. Will you give me another chance? I'll spend the rest of my life making this up to you."

Her bottom lip quivered.

"I love you." He said it again.

She swallowed hard.

"I need you."

Squeezing her eyes shut, he knew she fought more tears.

"I'm sorry, Isabel. It's unfair of me to pressure you like this." His voice quivered. "I just had to try." He kissed her forehead. "God be with you." When he turned toward the horses, she grabbed hold of his arm.

"What if tomorrow comes, and you don't want me anymore?"

He gazed into the teary eyes of the woman he loved with all his heart. "I promise I will want you every tomorrow for the rest of our lives." He drew her into his embrace and held her tight in his arms. "Take a chance on me, Isabel."

She sniffed.

"Take a chance that I'm the great adventure God has planned for your life."

She raised her head and looked into his eyes. Holding her

face between his hands, he kissed her, praying all the tenderness, all the love, all the hope would be transmitted to her. Her dazed gaze when the kiss ended spurred him on. He had to find the right words. She yearned to stay; he knew that much.

"If I'd not run ahead of God, if I'd waited for His plan and His timing, I'd never have hurt you. Sin does that, Isabel. Sin hurts innocent people. I loved you so much, so I just said what my heart felt. That was what got me into trouble." He paused. "Even if you still choose to leave, please forgive me."

"I'm not leaving, Slade, and I do forgive you." Her smile nearly undid him.

He closed his eyes and drew her against his chest, thanking God for His faithfulness. "Will you marry me, Isabel?"

"I will marry you, Slade." Her words carried a smile.

They kissed again.

He took her hand, and they walked back toward the horses. "You need to know, I always wanted you and loved you. I never changed my mind about those things."

"I realize that now, but I assumed you couldn't wait to get rid of me. I thought the happiest day of your life would be sending me home. After all, I seemed to cause you trouble no matter which way I turned."

Slade chuckled. "That you did, Miss Fairchild. That you did. But your perception is so far from the truth. Your leaving was killing me inside. I guess we should have been more honest about what we were thinking and feeling. Maybe things between us wouldn't have been so confused."

He untied Lady's reins and handed them to Isabel. She wrapped her arms around the mare's neck. "I'm back," she whispered near the horse's ear.

"Exactly why did you decide to leave? Because you thought I wanted you to?"

Isabel shook her head. "Because I loved you so much I couldn't bear to stay."

He closed his eyes and savored her words. Groaning, he pulled her to him. "Tell me again, Isabel."

She drew her brows together. "Tell you what?"

"Tell me you love me. You've never said it before."

She smiled, her playful, dimpled smile. "I love you, Slade Stanfield. I love you!" She turned to a couple passing by. "I love this man."

They smiled and nodded and obviously thought she was touched.

She held his head and stared deep into his eyes. "I love you. Today, tomorrow, and forever." She sealed her promise with a kiss.

epilogue

A month later in the Stanfields' church in San Diego, Isabel Fairchild and Susannah Stanfield walked down the aisle toward the men they loved. Both were dressed in beautiful gowns of white, Susannah in her mother's gown and Isabel in a borrowed one. Isabel thought of the marriage supper of the lamb she'd just read about in her Bible. After reading that text, the rich symbolism of her wedding meant so much more.

They moved slowly toward Slade and Dusty. Today, Susannah floated more than she limped.

At the sight of Slade, Isabel's heart leaped. He smiled, and she smiled back. *I thank You, Lord, for Slade. He not only loves me, but he appreciates me.*

When they reached the end of the aisle, Dusty took Susannah's arm and lifted her up the steps. Slade threaded Isabel's arm through his, and they joined Dusty and Susannah at the top of the steps. The love in Slade's eyes, the look on his face made Isabel's heart melt into a puddle of devotion. She hoped he never quit gazing at her with that delight in his expression.

The minister stood before them and talked about the covenant of marriage—a vow made before God. He spoke of the seriousness of the commitment they made not only to each other, but also to God Himself. And then he said the words she'd longed to hear. "Do you, Isabel Fairchild, take this man. . . ?" She did. A thousand times she did. After Slade, Susannah, and Dusty each took their turn, the minister said,

"I pronounce you, Slade and Isabel, and you, Dusty and Susannah, man and wife. You may kiss your brides."

Slowly, carefully, Slade lifted the veil. His eyes told her he cherished her. Inch by inch, he moved closer for the kiss. At last, his lips touched hers and ignited a longing within her to know him in every way. To truly be his wife.

"I have a surprise for you, Isabel," he told her on their way back down the aisle. "I'm taking you to San Francisco next week."

She stopped. Dusty and Susannah ran into them from behind. "San Francisco? To see my family?"

"Mr. Ochoa lent me a couple of men to help Dusty keep things running while we're gone."

She hugged him tight, thanking God again for this thoughtful husband of hers.

The following week they took the stage to Los Angeles, where they caught the train up the coast to San Francisco. They planned on surprising her family, so they arrived in the city on Saturday and spent the night in a hotel. Isabel knew that after church Gabrielle and Magdalene would bring their families to share Sunday dinner with Mother and Father. They'd each take a dish, and Isabel's nieces and nephews would be running all over the place, playing loudly. It had become tradition. Her heart longed to see each of them.

After she and Slade attended church, they paid a visit to the little cottage by the sea. Bobby ran to her first, giving her a hug. Then he ran to the house, shouting, "Aunt Izzy is home." Within seconds, the entire family surrounded Isabel and Slade.

After hugs and tears, Isabel introduced them to Slade. Then she proceeded to tell them the whole story of the last five months of her life. When she got to the best part, inviting Christ into her life, she looked her two sisters and her parents each in the eye and asked forgiveness. After more tears, they spent the day celebrating Isabel and Slade's marriage.

The entire family seemed to like him, especially Isabel's father. Slade liked them, too. Isabel could tell. But more important, Slade liked her, loved her, valued her, appreciated her, and adored her. And she felt the same about him. How glad she was she'd surrendered to the Lord and to this man's love. Life had never looked or felt better. Her adventure had just begun, and it had started with a surrendered heart.

A Letter To Our Readers

Dear Reader:

In order that we might better contribute to your reading enjoyment, we would appreciate your taking a few minutes to respond to the following questions. We welcome your comments and read each form and letter we receive. When completed, please return to the following:

Fiction Editor
Heartsong Presents
PO Box 719
Uhrichsville, Ohio 44683

1. Did you enjoy reading *Surrendered Heart* by Jeri Odell?
   - ❑ Very much! I would like to see more books by this author!
   - ❑ Moderately. I would have enjoyed it more if

   ____

   ____

   ____

2. Are you a member of **Heartsong Presents**? ❑ Yes ❑ No
   If no, where did you purchase this book? ______________

   ____

3. How would you rate, on a scale from 1 (poor) to 5 (superior), the cover design? ______________

4. On a scale from 1 (poor) to 10 (superior), please rate the following elements.

____ Heroine	____ Plot
____ Hero	____ Inspirational theme
____ Setting	____ Secondary characters

5. These characters were special because?________________

____

____

6. How has this book inspired your life?________________

____

____

7. What settings would you like to see covered in future **Heartsong Presents** books? ________________

____

____

8. What are some inspirational themes you would like to see treated in future books? ________________

____

____

9. Would you be interested in reading other **Heartsong Presents** titles? ❑ Yes ❑ No

10. Please check your age range:

❑ Under 18 ❑ 18-24

❑ 25-34 ❑ 35-45

❑ 46-55 ❑ Over 55

Name____

Occupation ___________________________________

Address _____________________________________

City________________ State______ Zip__________

FRONTIER BRIDES

4 stories in 1

Four romances ride through the sagebrush of yesteryear by Colleen L. Reece.

Reece shares the compelling stories of people who put their lives on the line to develop a new land. . .and new love.

Historical, paperback, 464 pages, 5 3/16"x 8"

♥ ♥ ♥ ♥ ♥ ♥ ♥ ♥ ♥ ♥ ♥ ♥ ♥ ♥ ♥ ♥ ♥

Please send me ____ copies of *Frontier Brides.* I am enclosing $6.97 for each. (Please add $2.00 to cover postage and handling per order. OH add 7% tax.)

Send check or money order, no cash or C.O.D.s please.

Name ______________________________

Address ______________________________

City, State, Zip ______________________________

To place a credit card order, call 1-800-847-8270.

Send to: Heartsong Presents Reader Service, PO Box 721, Uhrichsville, OH 44683

♥ ♥ ♥ ♥ ♥ ♥ ♥ ♥ ♥ ♥ ♥ ♥ ♥ ♥ ♥ ♥ ♥

Heartsong

HISTORICAL ROMANCE IS CHEAPER BY THE DOZEN!

Buy any assortment of twelve *Heartsong Presents* titles and save 25% off of the already discounted price of $2.97 each!

*plus $2.00 shipping and handling per order and sales tax where applicable.

HEARTSONG PRESENTS TITLES AVAILABLE NOW:

__HP259 *Five Geese Flying*, T. Peterson
__HP260 *The Will and the Way*, D. Pace
__HP263 *The Starfire Quilt*, A. Allen
__HP264 *Journey Toward Home*, C. Cox
__HP271 *Where Leads the Heart*, C. Coble
__HP272 *Albert's Destiny*, B. L. Etchision
__HP275 *Along Unfamiliar Paths*, A. Rognlie
__HP279 *An Unexpected Love*, A. Boeshaar
__HP299 *Em's Only Chance*, R. Dow
__HP300 *Changes of the Heart*, J. M. Miller
__HP303 *Maid of Honor*, C. R. Scheidies
__HP304 *Song of the Cimarron*, K. Stevens
__HP307 *Silent Stranger*, P. Darty
__HP308 *A Different Kind of Heaven*, T. Shuttlesworth
__HP319 *Margaret's Quest*, M. Chapman
__HP320 *Hope in the Great Southland*, M. Hawkins
__HP323 *No More Sea*, G. Brandt
__HP324 *Love in the Great Southland*, M. Hawkins
__HP327 *Plains of Promise*, C. Coble
__HP331 *A Man for Libby*, J. A. Grote
__HP332 *Hidden Trails*, J. B. Schneider
__HP339 *Birdsong Road*, M. L. Colln
__HP340 *Lone Wolf*, L. Lough
__HP343 *Texas Rose*, D. W. Smith
__HP344 *The Measure of a Man*, C. Cox
__HP351 *Courtin' Patience*, K. Comeaux
__HP352 *After the Flowers Fade*, A. Rognlie
__HP356 *Texas Lady*, D. W. Smith
__HP363 *Rebellious Heart*, R. Druten
__HP371 *Storm*, D. L. Christner
__HP372 *'Til We Meet Again*, P. Griffin
__HP380 *Neither Bond Nor Free*, N. C. Pykare
__HP384 *Texas Angel*, D. W. Smith
__HP387 *Grant Me Mercy*, J. Stengl
__HP388 *Lessons in Love*, N. Lavo
__HP392 *Healing Sarah's Heart*, T. Shuttlesworth
__HP395 *To Love a Stranger*, C. Coble
__HP400 *Susannah's Secret*, K. Comeaux
__HP403 *The Best Laid Plans*, C. M. Parker
__HP407 *Sleigh Bells*, J. M. Miller
__HP408 *Destinations*, T. H. Murray
__HP411 *Spirit of the Eagle*, G. Fields
__HP412 *To See His Way*, K. Paul
__HP415 *Sonoran Sunrise*, N. J. Farrier
__HP416 *Both Sides of the Easel*, B. Youree
__HP419 *Captive Heart*, D. Mindrup
__HP420 *In the Secret Place*, P. Griffin
__HP423 *Remnant of Forgiveness*, S. Laity
__HP424 *Darling Cassidy*, T. V. Bateman
__HP427 *Remnant of Grace*, S. K. Downs
__HP428 *An Unmasked Heart*, A. Boeshaar
__HP431 *Myles from Anywhere*, J. Stengl
__HP432 *Tears in a Bottle*, G. Fields
__HP435 *Circle of Vengeance*, M. J. Conner
__HP436 *Marty's Ride*, M. Davis
__HP439 *One With the Wind*, K. Stevens
__HP440 *The Stranger's Kiss*, Y. Lehman
__HP443 *Lizzy's Hope*, L. A. Coleman
__HP444 *The Prodigal's Welcome*, K. Billerbeck
__HP447 *Viking Pride*, D. Mindrup
__HP448 *Chastity's Angel*, L. Ford
__HP451 *Southern Treasures*, L. A. Coleman
__HP452 *Season of Hope*, C. Cox
__HP455 *My Beloved Waits*, P. Darty
__HP456 *The Cattle Baron's Bride*, C. Coble
__HP459 *Remnant of Light*, T. James
__HP460 *Sweet Spring*, M. H. Flinkman
__HP463 *Crane's Bride*, L. Ford
__HP464 *The Train Stops Here*, G. Sattler
__HP467 *Hidden Treasures*, J. Odell
__HP468 *Tarah's Lessons*, T. V. Bateman
__HP471 *One Man's Honor*, L. A. Coleman
__HP472 *The Sheriff and the Outlaw*, K. Comeaux
__HP475 *Bittersweet Bride*, D. Hunter
__HP476 *Hold on My Heart*, J. A. Grote

(If ordering from this page, please remember to include it with the order form.)

Presents

__HP479 *Cross My Heart,* C. Cox
__HP480 *Sonoran Star,* N. J. Farrier
__HP483 *Forever Is Not Long Enough,* B. Youree
__HP484 *The Heart Knows,* E. Bonner
__HP488 *Sonoran Sweetheart,* N. J. Farrier
__HP491 *An Unexpected Surprise,* R. Dow
__HP492 *The Other Brother,* L. N. Dooley
__HP495 *With Healing in His Wings,* S. Krueger
__HP496 *Meet Me with a Promise,* J. A. Grote
__HP499 *Her Name Was Rebekah,* B. K. Graham
__HP500 *Great Southland Gold,* M. Hawkins
__HP503 *Sonoran Secret,* N. J. Farrier
__HP504 *Mail-Order Husband,* D. Mills
__HP507 *Trunk of Surprises,* D. Hunt
__HP508 *Dark Side of the Sun,* R. Druten
__HP511 *To Walk in Sunshine,* S. Laity
__HP512 *Precious Burdens,* C. M. Hake
__HP515 *Love Almost Lost,* I. B. Brand
__HP516 *Lucy's Quilt,* J. Livingston
__HP519 *Red River Bride,* C. Coble
__HP520 *The Flame Within,* P. Griffin
__HP523 *Raining Fire,* L. A. Coleman
__HP524 *Laney's Kiss,* T. V. Bateman
__HP531 *Lizzie,* L. Ford
__HP532 *A Promise Made,* J. L. Barton
__HP535 *Viking Honor,* D. Mindrup
__HP536 *Emily's Place,* T. V. Bateman
__HP539 *Two Hearts Wait,* F. Chrisman
__HP540 *Double Exposure,* S. Laity
__HP543 *Cora,* M. Colvin
__HP544 *A Light Among Shadows,* T. H. Murray
__HP547 *Maryelle,* L. Ford
__HP548 *His Brother's Bride,* D. Hunter
__HP551 *Healing Heart,* R. Druten
__HP552 *The Vicar's Daughter,* K. Comeaux
__HP555 *But For Grace,* T. V. Bateman
__HP556 *Red Hills Stranger,* M. G. Chapman
__HP559 *Banjo's New Song,* R. Dow
__HP560 *Heart Appearances,* P. Griffin
__HP563 *Redeemed Hearts,* C. M. Hake
__HP564 *Tender Hearts,* K. Dykes
__HP567 *Summer Dream,* M. H. Flinkman
__HP568 *Loveswept,* T. H. Murray
__HP571 *Bayou Fever,* K. Y'Barbo
__HP572 *Temporary Husband,* D. Mills
__HP575 *Kelly's Chance,* W. E. Brunstetter
__HP576 *Letters from the Enemy,* S. M. Warren
__HP579 *Grace,* L. Ford
__HP580 *Land of Promise,* C. Cox
__HP583 *Ramshakle Rose,* C. M. Hake
__HP584 *His Brother's Castoff,* L. N. Dooley
__HP587 *Lilly's Dream,* P. Darty
__HP588 *Torey's Prayer,* T. V. Bateman
__HP591 *Eliza,* M. Colvin
__HP592 *Refining Fire,* C. Cox

Great Inspirational Romance at a Great Price!

Heartsong Presents books are inspirational romances in contemporary and historical settings, designed to give you an enjoyable, spirit-lifting reading experience. You can choose wonderfully written titles from some of today's best authors like Peggy Darty, Sally Laity, Tracie Peterson, Colleen L. Reece, Debra White Smith, and many others.

When ordering quantities less than twelve, above titles are $2.97 each.
Not all titles may be available at time of order.

SEND TO: **Heartsong Presents** Reader's Service
P.O. Box 721, Uhrichsville, Ohio 44683

Please send me the items checked above. I am enclosing $ ______
(please add $2.00 to cover postage per order. OH add 7% tax. NJ add 6%.). Send check or money order, no cash or C.O.D.s, please.

To place a credit card order, call 1-800-847-8270.

NAME ______________________________

ADDRESS ______________________________

CITY/STATE ____________________ ZIP ________

HPS 7-04

HEARTSONG ❤ PRESENTS

Love Stories Are Rated G!

That's for godly, gratifying, and of course, great! If you love a thrilling love story but don't appreciate the sordidness of some popular paperback romances, **Heartsong Presents** is for you. In fact, **Heartsong Presents** is the premiere inspirational romance book club featuring love stories where Christian faith is the primary ingredient in a marriage relationship.

Sign up today to receive your first set of four, never-before-published Christian romances. Send no money now; you will receive a bill with the first shipment. You may cancel at any time without obligation, and if you aren't completely satisfied with any selection, you may return the books for an immediate refund!

Imagine. . .four new romances every four weeks—two historical, two contemporary—with men and women like you who long to meet the one God has chosen as the love of their lives. . .all for the low price of $10.99 postpaid.

To join, simply complete the coupon below and mail to the address provided. **Heartsong Presents** romances are rated G for another reason: They'll arrive Godspeed!

YES! Sign me up for Hearts❤ng!

NEW MEMBERSHIPS WILL BE SHIPPED IMMEDIATELY!
Send no money now. We'll bill you only $10.99 postpaid with your first shipment of four books. Or for faster action, call toll free 1-800-847-8270.

NAME ______________________________

ADDRESS ______________________________

CITY ______________ STATE ______ ZIP ______

MAIL TO: HEARTSONG PRESENTS, P.O. Box 721, Uhrichsville, Ohio 44683
or visit www.heartsongpresents.com